Books by Tristan Bancks

The Tom Weekly series

My Life and Other Stuff I Made Up

My Life and Other Stuff that Went Wrong

My Life and Other Massive Mistakes

My Life and Other Exploding Chickens

My Life and Other Weaponised Muffins

My Life and Other Failed Experiments

Two Wolves

The Fall

The Mac Slater series

Mac Slater, Coolhunter

Mac Slater, Imaginator

TOM WEEKLY

MY LIFE AND OTHER

FAILED EXPERIMENTS

AS TOLD TO
TRISTAN BANCKS AND
GUS GORDON

RANDOM HOUSE AUSTRALIA

A Random House book
Published by Penguin Random House Australia Pty Ltd
Level 3, 100 Pacific Highway, North Sydney NSW 2060
www.penguin.com.au

Penguin
Random House
Australia

First published by Random House Australia in 2018

A catalogue record for this
book is available from the
National Library of Australia

NATIONAL
LIBRARY
OF AUSTRALIA

ISBN: 978 0 14378 161 5

Cover and internal illustrations by Gus Gordon
Cover design by Astred Hicks, designcherry
Internal design by Benjamin Fairclough © Penguin Random House Australia,
based on original series design by Astred Hicks, designcherry
Printed in Australia by Griffin Press, an accredited ISO AS/NZS 14001:2004
Environmental Management System printer

Random House Australia uses papers that are natural, renewable and
recyclable products and made from wood grown in sustainable forests.
The logging and manufacturing processes are expected to conform to the
environmental regulations of the country of origin.

Contents

Hey.

I'm Tom Weekly, and my life is a science experiment gone horribly wrong. Things never quite turn out the way I want them to, but my new motto is, 'Never give up, never give in.' No matter what life throws at me — whether it's a rock-hard fruitcake or a headbutt in a very bad place, getting attacked by a gang of killer possums, eating a car or being rejected in public by the woman I love, I'm going to look on the bright side.

Wish me luck . . . I'm going in.

Tom

Hostage

'Give me all your money or the guinea pig gets it.'

These are the first words I hear when I arrive home from school. I'm standing in my bedroom doorway. My evil sister, Tanya, is holding Gus, my brand-new guinea pig, out the window. Gus has long, ginger hair. He paws at the air with his tiny claws.

'What did you say?' I ask.

'I said give me all your money or I drop your guinea pig onto the concrete.'

It's at least a three-metre drop to the path below. I've always known my sister was evil. She once threw a hamburger patty at my head. She's used me as a slave for at least four years of my childhood. She made me eat

This is GUS.

He's been kidnapped by a truly evil, maniacal psycho—my sister!

Vegemite off her big toe. But to threaten to take the life of the world's cutest guinea pig? This is a new low.

So I say the obvious thing: 'I don't have any money.'

'LIAR!' she shouts, almost making Gus's black marble eyes pop out of his head.

'Put. Him. Down!' I demand, dropping my school bag to the floor.

'If you say so,' she says, shrugging.

'No!' I rush forward.

'I thought you said put him down?' she says, all innocent.

'Give him to me *now*,' I demand in a low growl.

'Be a good little boy,' she says. 'Unlock your trapdoor and give me your money, then you can have the ranga back.'

I've warned her not to call Gus a 'ranga'. It's not nice to make fun of people with red hair. Or guinea pigs.

'I'm going to the movies with Bella in fifteen minutes and I need cash,' she says. 'So make it snappy.'

Gus swings in the breeze, his eyes pleading with me to follow her instructions very, very carefully. But I can't. Listening to Tanya is against my religion. And every hostage movie I've ever seen has taught me one thing: don't give in to the evil kidnapper's demands.

Sweat trickles from my forehead and into my eye. I wipe it.

I need time to think.

I kneel down and peel back the edge of the rug in the middle of my bedroom floor.

I roll it back to reveal my trapdoor – a small, square hole in the floor, about a school ruler wide and long. It is secured with a flat, gold padlock.

I glare up at Tanya. I take one of the keys from the string around my neck. I open the padlock. She and Gus watch closely. I lift the lid. It stops Tanya from seeing what's inside – all my worldly possessions:

- four-and-a-half packets of Wizz Fizz
- a small tub of premium quality homemade slime
- a long cardboard pack of sparklers
- a book of horror stories that Mum says I'm too young to read
- a hundred water bombs
- a pre-licked giant lollypop in cling wrap
- a small, black cashbox.

The cashbox has my birthday money in it: $50 from Nan, $50 from Mum, $80 from kids at my party and some loose change. My entire fortune. I'm saving for a bike, so there's no way I'm giving Tanya $180. Think of everything I could do with that kind of bankroll. Gus only cost me five bucks at the pet shop. I could buy another 36 guinea pigs for $180 and set up a guinea pig farm. I could milk them and start a new hipster craze for guinea pig milk. I could tell everyone that it's a superfood with mysterious healing qualities, and they could extend their lives by putting it in their cappuccinos.

I look over the lid, into Gus's eyes, and I know that my dreams of being a guinea

Do you know how hard it is to milk a Guinea Pig?

pig milk billionaire can never be realised. I love Gus. I could buy every guinea pig in the world and I'd never find another one like him. He's smart, sensitive and loyal. He understands me in a way that only a guinea pig could.

'My fingers are getting mighty slippery,' Tanya taunts.

'Gus is my friend.'

'Well, that's embarrassing. He's only half a step up from being a rat.'

She's talking about Rarnalda, my pet rat who's been missing for two months. I fear that Mum may have taken her for a long ride out into the bush. A rat-napping. I bought Gus to heal the wound left by Rarnalda's sudden and mysterious disappearance.

'*Gus*,' I tell her. 'His name is *Gus*.' I figure reminding her that he has a name might make her care more.

'"Pus", did you say?' she asks. 'Nice name. It suits him.'

I look back down into my trapdoor. I jingle some coins like I'm counting money.

'I have a dollar sixty,' I tell her.

'That's a lie.'

'No, it's not. You can come have a look if you like.'

Tanya thinks about it for a moment. To look inside the trapdoor she'll have to move away from the window, then I'll tackle her, grab Gus and throw *her* out the window.

'Nice try,' she says. 'You got tons of cash for your birthday.'

'I spent it.'

'On what?'

'Stuff.'

'What stuff?'

'Lollies,' I say.

'You bought $200 worth of lollies?'

'It was only $180,' I say.

'Oh, sorry. Because $180 is a reasonable amount of money to spend on lollies. Give me the money *now*.'

'I told you, I –'

'Gus doesn't want you to lie, Tommy. And my arm's getting *real* tired.'

Gus isn't even struggling now. He's just hanging there, swinging back and forth like a pendulum. He's given up hope. I'm the only one who can save him from the clutches of Tanya – the Death Eater of the guinea pig universe.

'Okay, you got me,' I say. 'I have $5.35.' I avoid round numbers, hoping that the randomness of $5.35 will trick her into thinking that's all I have. I mean, how could I come up with a number like that just off the top of my head? Sometimes I amaze myself.

'That's it!' she screams.

'Okay,' I say. 'Relax. Sheesh. Sensitive.'

'Ten seconds,' she says. 'Ten . . . nine . . .'

She looks serious now. I figure I have three options.

1) Dive into my trapdoor, scramble beneath the house, drag the rusty slippery dip under the window, and when Tanya drops Gus he'll go, 'Wheeeee!' and slide to safety.

'Seven . . . six . . .'

2) Give her a brown paper bag stuffed with Wizz Fizz wrappers and tell her it's cash.

'Five . . . four . . .' Gus gives me one last pitiful stare.

3) Tell her that Gus *is* my piggy bank, that he ate the money to hide it for me and that it's inside him. So if she drops Gus she'll be throwing away the cash.

'Three . . . two . . .'

Then it hits me. The perfect way out of this predicament.

'One,' Tanya announces. 'Bye-bye, Pus. Nice knowing you.'

At the last moment, just as Tanya goes to drop Gus, I grab the edge of the rug and pull hard. Tanya's feet slip out from under her. She screams, her hip hits the windowsill, and she goes flying out. Gus does, too.

They squeal as they fall.

What have I done?

I rush to the window. I hear the impact. I close my eyes and squeeze them tight. I don't want to

see what's happened. What if Gus fell faster than Tanya and was squished beneath her? What if Tanya fell faster than Gus and I've put an end to my only sister? I'd have to go to jail and wear orange prison overalls for the rest of my life. Orange really isn't my colour.

I open one eye and look down. What I see surprises me.

Tanya is lying on her back, on top of the garbage bins parked on the path. Her head is on the recycling, her hips on the garbage and her legs are in the open green bin with all the compost and grass clippings. The bin lids are dented, but she's only fallen half of the three metres to the path. Her eyes are open.

'You're alive!' I say.

'You're dead,' she says.

But I'm more worried about Gus. I can't see him. Did she squish him? Has he run away?

Just then I see one furry paw. Then another, clawing out from beneath a rockmelon skin in the compost bin. It's him!

'Gus!' I shout as his nose comes into view. 'Hey, little buddy.'

Gus squirms all the way out as Tanya sits up.

I think quick, look around and lower my long, dark-blue curtain out the window. It hovers just above the bin.

'Jump on!' I urge.

Gus doesn't need to be told twice. He leaps up, digs his little claws into the bottom of the curtain and I reel him up. It's like a helicopter rescue at sea.

As Gus is pulled to safety Tanya reaches out and makes one last snatch for him. Gus poops with fear and the nuggets fall directly into Tanya's open mouth.

She squeals and spits, clawing at her tongue. 'That's IT!' she shrieks, just as the garbage bin lid collapses and she falls in, squelching deep down into the rubbish.

The doorbell rings.

'That must be Bella,' I say. 'I'll let her know you're feeling a bit rubbish.'

'Nooooo!' Tanya calls.

I peel Gus's claws off the curtain and cuddle him into my chest. I brush some bits of rockmelon out of his fur, close my window, lock it and secure my trapdoor. Somehow, I've managed to hold onto my money, save my precious guinea pig's life and do away with my evil sister all in one swift pull of a rug. I click my heels as Gus and I head off into the kitchen for a celebratory snack. Hostage situations sure make you hungry.

Tom Weekly

Hostage negotiator extraordinaire

Tom Weekly's
Must-Read List
of Weird Stuff
About Guinea Pigs

I love facts — weird facts, funny facts, gross facts.
They reckon truth is stranger than fiction.
You'll believe that after you read my list of
freaky guinea pig factoids.

* Guinea pigs are not related to pigs at all,
  but female guinea pigs are known as 'sows'
  and males are 'boars'. The babies are not
  guinea piglets, though – they're 'pups'.
  And, in the wild, they used to travel in
  'herds'. (I've seen a video of a guinea pig
  stampede. Terrifying.)

A Guinea pig stampede

* Guinea pigs are actually related to capybaras, which are the largest living rodents. Capybaras can grow up to 1.3 metres long and 60 centimetres tall! Let's hope they don't get any ideas about world domination. One of my greatest fears is being eaten alive by an extra-large guinea pig.

* For thousands of years tribal people in South America have eaten guinea pigs and, in recent years, they've shown up on plates in fancy South American restaurants around the world. My motto is: 'Never eat a guinea pig unless you want a capybara to eat you.'

* Another name for a guinea pig is a 'cavy'. This is short for their scientific name *Cavia porcellus*. 'Porcellus' is Latin for 'little pig'. According to Wookieepedia (a Star Wars fan site), Porcellus was also the head chef in Jabba's palace on Tatooine in *Return of the Jedi*. I hope Cavy Bolognese wasn't on the menu.

* When a guinea pig is excited it jumps up and down. This is called 'popcorning'.

* The Guinness World Record for 'Longest Jump by a Guinea Pig' is held by Truffles, a Scottish guinea pig, who leapt 48 centimetres (almost half a metre!) on 6 April 2012. And the fastest guinea pig on the planet? Flash, a guinea pig from London, who ran 10 metres in 8.81 seconds on 27 July 2009. Dare you to train your G.P. to beat those amazing 'feets'.

* An ancient civilization in Peru worshipped guinea pigs, and often included them in their artwork. I bet you didn't know you had furry royalty living in your hutch.

* And how about this little-known fact? Guinea pigs eat poo pellets directly from their own bottoms, like a candy dispenser. This is normal for a guinea pig and is known as 'coprophagy'. Sometimes they pull this sick trick 200 times a day. When they're feeling ill, they steal and eat poop from other guinea pigs' bottoms, too. At least they're recycling, I guess.

'Popcorning'
(or Guinea Pig
break-dancing)

Sources: petsforhomes.co.uk, onlineguineapigcare.com, calicavycollective.com, guinnessworldrecords.com

Author Visit

'We are *very* lucky to have a special visitor
to the school today,' Mr Skroop, our deputy
principal, announces. He's standing on stage
at the front of the assembly hall.

Skroop is tall and skinny, and he has
leftover food in his teeth. (Possibly bits of
the small children he ate for breakfast.)
He wears a black suit and a thin grey tie.
The very special visitor is standing next to
him. He is jolly-looking, with a silver beard
and a 'Reading is Fun' t-shirt.

Author, Barry Cheese

'As a special treat we have invited the *entire school* and I *know* that you will all be on your *best* behaviour,' he says with a threatening glare. 'No chit-chat. No laughter. No silly questions.'

The kindy kids are on the floor up front, wriggling and writhing. The primary kids are on chairs. Jack and I are up near the back.

'Our guest is a *real live* author who writes *books*,' Skroop continues. 'His name is . . .'

Skroop scans the piece of paper in his hand. He looks uncertain.

The author leans in and whispers something in Skroop's ear.

'Barry Cheese,' Skroop announces.

The author leans in again and whispers something else. Skroop whispers something back and the author nods.

'I'm sorry. Gary Cleese!' Skroop corrects.

Jack and I snigger. Kids whisper and giggle.

Skroop, red-faced, raises his voice. '*If* I am embarrassed by student behaviour, there *will* be severe and immediate consequences. Do I make myself clear?'

'Yes, Mis-ter Skroop,' we all chime.

'Excellent,' he says. 'Well, without further ado, I would like to welcome Mr Chee . . . Cleese!'

Skroop hands over the microphone and hurries down the stairs at the front of the stage.

'Hello, children!' the author says, his eyes wide. 'How are we all today?'

Kids mutter:

'Good.'

'Not bad.'

'Okay.'

'Alright.'

'Been better.'

The author shuffles in place before pasting a wide grin across his face. 'Are we ready to have some fun in the wonderful world of books and reading?'

A kindy kid up front raises his hand. The author points at him. 'Yes?'

'Do you have a cat?' the kid asks.

'Um . . . no, I don't have a cat. My son, however, has a guinea pig.'

Another few kindergarten hands shoot up. The author points to another kid.

'My cousin had a guinea pig. Its name was Brussels Sprout.'

'That's fantastic!' the author says. 'We all know the importance of vegetables to a well-balanced –'

'It died.'

'Oh.'

Jack laughs. I don't think he means to. He doesn't have anything against guinea pigs. Skroop narrows his brows to let Jack know that Brussels Sprout's death is no laughing matter.

'That's very sad,' the author says. 'But, today, I'm here to talk to you about books.

Specifically, my books.' He points to the five books he has set up on the table out front. They look like fantasy novels. I can make out a serpent-man on the cover of one and a unicorn-woman on another . . . and maybe a sword-wielding dragon on another.

A girl's hand shoots up right in front of him. From year two, I think.

'Yes? What's your question?' the author asks.

'Do you think books are more important than guinea pigs?'

'Well, guinea pigs are friends for a time, but a good book will last you a lifetime.' He smiles.

'You don't care about Lenny's dead guinea pig!' she accuses.

'Not *my* dead guinea pig,' Lenny says. 'My *cousin's*.'

The author looks up to the teachers for help, but they seem perfectly happy to see someone else in the line of fire for once.

'I'm actually writing a story about a guinea pig at the moment!' he says, which gets everyone's attention. 'Maybe you can help me write it and I'll thank your school in the back of the book.' He picks up a marker and writes 'Guinea Pig Story' on the whiteboard.

'Why should we write the book for you?' a red-headed boy on the floor calls out.

'I just thought it'd be –'

'Can you split the profits with us?' the boy asks.

'Well, the thing is, there won't *be* many profits. See, if the price of a book is a pie, I get one slice of pie and the publisher and

bookseller and other people who help make
the book, they get nine slices.'

'What kind of pie?' a kid yells out.

'Are you rich or poor?'

'Well, neither really.'

'My dad wrote a book of dad jokes, but he
only sold nine copies,' says the redhead.

'Are you famous?' a girl asks.

'Not really, no. Only to people who read
my books and –'

'Is the guinea pig in your story dead?'
a year two girl calls out.

'Well . . .'

'NO more calling out!' Skroop shouts
from the side of the hall. '*Listen* to our
very special guest, but no silly questions.
Understood?'

'Yes, Mis-ter Skroop,' we all chant.

The year two girl who asked about the dead guinea pig starts to cry, and the kids next to her put their arms around her. A wave of chatter washes over the room.

'What could we name our guinea pig in the story?' the author asks, trying to redirect attention.

Kids are wriggling now.

The Adventures of ROGER, the Dead Guinea Pig

by Barry Cheese

A classic for the ages

'Pickles!' someone calls out.

'Murgatroyd,' says another kid.

'Jeff!'

A year three girl, Emily Pearce, puts up her hand.

'Yes!' the author asks.

'Have you ever seen an emoo?'

'An emoo?' the author asks.

'She means an emu,' the girl next to her says. 'She's American. That's the way she says it.'

'Oh! Yes, I have seen an emoo – I mean an emu. But . . . we're talking about a guinea pig. Now, what happens to our guinea pig named Murgatroyd?'

Jonah Flem, an annoying kid in my year, has his hand up. The author ignores him.

'Who has an idea?' he repeats, scanning the audience.

'Jonah does,' Brent Bunder says with an idiotic grin, pointing at his friend.

The author takes a breath and waves his hand at Jonah. 'Yes. What's your idea?'

'We should call the guinea pig Mister Sparkles, and he's made of fireworks, and every time he farts fireworks shoot out of his you-know-what, and then a unicorn comes down from Unicorn Land and eats his brain.'

The author forces a smile. 'Thank you, Jonah. Very creative,' he says. 'Any other ideas?' I notice that he doesn't put Jonah's genius suggestion up on the board. 'Okay, look, this isn't working. Why don't we move on and I'll read you a chapter from one of my books?'

One of the kindy kids puts her hand up and waves it around like crazy.

One of my favourites.

'Let me see,' says the author, paging
through his book, trying to ignore her.
'Chapter four . . .'

The girl's arm is going to come off if she
waves it any harder.

'Yes, what?' the author snaps.

'She just pulled out my tooth.' She points at the grinning girl next to her.

'Really?' he asks, looking at the tiny nub in Grinning Girl's hand and the blood trickling down the girl's arm. He looks up at Mr Skroop. 'I think she actually did pull her tooth out.'

Mr Skroop tiptoes through the audience, saying, 'Sorry. Excuse me. Sorry.' He grabs the girl who lost the tooth under the armpits, lifts her up, grabs the amateur dentist's arm and leads them out of the hall through the side door. As soon as Skroop leaves, thirty kids' hands shoot up. Their teachers try to get them to settle, but the kids can't be stopped.

'Does your hand get sore when you're writing a book?' a kid yells out.

'Do you have a wife?'

'Do your books stink?'

'Do you dream in colour?'

'Mister, you have something in your nose.'

The author wipes his nose.

'Other side,' the girl calls out.

The author looks embarrassed and kind of picks his nose.

Kids start to giggle.

'You got it,' the girl says.

He seems to flick something onto the floor.

'Right . . .' the author says. 'Now, chapter four, "The Worst Day of My Life" . . .' He clears his throat to begin reading.

'Actually, half of it's still in there,' the girl says before a teacher leans over and plucks her out of the audience.

'No, let me go! It's not my fault he had a nostril nugget. Stop!'

The whole audience falls apart laughing. It's chaos.

'Oh, will you all BE QUIET!' the author screams.

His words echo off the walls of the hall.

The room drops to silence.

Everyone stares at the not-so-jolly-anymore author with the silver beard.

He's looking down at the floor, sweating, rattled.

Jack smiles.

I kick him.

I feel really bad for Gary Cleese. He's usually tucked away in his little office in his 'Reading is Fun' pyjamas writing a book, and now he's out in the world being forced to speak to humans, and we're wrecking everything for him. The whole audience

The moment author
Barry Cheese wished
he'd never visited
Kings Bay Public.

squirms. I hate seeing people feel embarrassed.
I want to help him. I have an idea how I can
save the day. My hand shoots up.

'Sir?'

'What?' he snips, looking up.

Kids in the audience turn to me.

'I really like your books.'

He stares at me for a moment. 'Really?'

'Yes,' I say. 'They're . . . amazing.'

His shoulders seem to relax ever so slightly.

'Which one have you read?' he asks.

My mind rattles through his talk so far. He hasn't mentioned any book titles, and I can't quite make out the titles on the books out front, so I say the obvious thing: 'All of them!'

He looks pleased. The deep creases between his brows start to smooth. A smile curls the edge of his mouth. 'That's . . . brilliant. Thank you. I appreciate it.' He turns to the audience. 'I'm very sorry, everyone, for losing my patience. I . . . don't get out much.'

Skroop is at the side of the hall again with the dentist and patient sitting on chairs next to him. He nods approvingly at me for saving the day. I might get a bronze award for this. I am a great humanitarian.

'Which was your favourite?' the author asks.

My head snaps back to the front. He's talking to me. He wants a specific book title. Why would he ask for that? I saved the day. He could just read his chapter and move on, but he has to ruin it by asking me which book, of all the ones I haven't read, I like best. Everyone's watching me. I have to come up with something. I'll look like a liar if I don't.

'They're all so good. Remind me, what's your most recent book?' I ask.

'*The Shadow Scrolls*,' he says.

'Yeah, that one. It's great.'

'It doesn't come out till next week. How did you manage to get hold of a copy?' he asks.

I glance at Jack. He's grinning, watching me drown. He knows that I haven't read any of this guy's books. Now I'm sweating. How did this happen? I was just trying to be nice – now I have 399 kids, 14 teachers and an angry author staring at me.

Jack can't believe what a liar I am.

Kids all around the hall mutter and giggle.

Skroop's nod has turned into a glare.

The author isn't smiling anymore.

'You haven't read any of my books,' he says, crestfallen. 'Have you?'

I shrink in my chair.

He turns and starts to pack up his books. 'NONE of you have! I swear this is the last time I visit a school.' He grabs his tatty leather bag and throws the books into it. 'I should start writing books for adults. I don't even *like* children! You're a bunch of greedy little snotty-nosed, question-asking, tooth-pulling liars. Do you hear me?'

Silence.

Mr Skroop dashes back onstage. 'Ah, thank you very much for your time. One of our students would just like to say a few words of gratitude.'

Desperate, Skroop looks into the crowd and points at me. 'Tom Weekly.'

Why would he do that? I just offended the guy, lied to him, and I'm hopeless at public speaking. But I'm scared of Skroop, so I stand and walk to the stage. Skroop lowers the mic for me.

I clear my throat and try to lick my lips but my mouth is as dry as the Sahara.

'Sorry about before,' I whisper to the author. He looks away, a sneer on his face.

I lean into the microphone. 'Um . . . thank you for coming to our school and . . . telling us so many interesting things about your books.'

I realise that he hasn't actually told us anything about his books. Except one.

'I especially liked the bit about the guinea pig,' I say nervously. 'Would everyone please, um, put your hands together for . . . Mister Barry Cheese!'

10 Funny Books

When I'm writing my stories I'm reading funny stuff, too. Here are ten of my fave funny books. If you have any other favourite funny books, hit me up at thetomweekly@gmail.com

1. *The Giggler Treatment*, Roddy Doyle

2. *The Twits*, Roald Dahl

3. *Tales of a Fourth Grade Nothing*, Judy Blume

4. *Toad Rage*, Morris Gleitzman

5. *The Bad Beginning*, Lemony Snicket

6. *The Stupendously Spectacular Spelling Bee*, Deborah Abela

7. *William*, Richmal Crompton

8. *Mr Bambuckle's Remarkables*, Tim Harris

9. *Marge in Charge*, Isla Fisher

10. *The Bad Guys*, Aaron Blabey

(And the other books about my life, of course!)

Razorblade Fruitcake

Nan pulls on her black balaclava – a woollen mask with eyeholes.

'I can't see a thing,' she says.

She has it on backwards. I help her twist it around.

'That's better,' she says. 'Thanks, love.'

She looks like a proper robber. Until she puts her spectacles on over the top.

'You sure you want to do this?' I whisper.

'You bet your bottom dollar I do.'

We're standing in a garden bed, pressed

up against the brick wall at the back of the
nursing home. It's 8.37 pm on a cold, clear
night. The window above us is open about
30 centimetres. It's quite a climb to get up
there, but we can smell what we came for –
a fruitcake. Steam rises from it and curls out
the window.

'Put your foot in here,' Nan says, knitting
her knobbly fingers together to give me a
boost.

'We really shouldn't be doing this,' I tell her.

'Why not? You're not *scared,* are you?'

'No, I'm not. It's just . . . wrong.'

'Poppycock,' she says. 'That's the problem
with kids these days. Bunch of do-gooders.
Always trying to be nice. Well, you don't
make it to the top of the fruitcake world by
being nice.'

'Why don't you just win fair and square?'
I ask. 'Your cake'll be the best anyway – you're
the reigning champ!'

'Can't risk it,' Nan says. 'She's threatened
to take away my crown. I won't be beaten by
that monstrous woman.'

'She's my best mate's grandmother.'

'She's a beast!' Nan hisses.

My nan and Jack's nan had actually
been getting along pretty well for once,

until Sue entered the competition. Now Nan's been banging on for weeks about how evil Sue is. I'm sick of it. I really don't want to lose my best mate over a fruitcake.

I sigh and peel off my balaclava. 'I'm sorry, Nan. You'll have to find someone else to do your dirty work.'

She grabs me by the front of my shirt. 'Don't you go anywhere.' She's so close I can smell her milky-tea breath. Twinings English Breakfast, if I'm not mistaken. Two sugars.

'Nan, I –'

'Do you want to know the *real* reason we're stealing the cake?' she asks.

'Why?'

'I didn't want to tell you.'

'Tell me what?'

'Forget it.'

'Please, Nan.'

'I shouldn't,' she says, looking down into the garden, poking a white flower with the toe of her shoe.

'Shouldn't what?'

'You're young and I want you to think that the world is a good and happy place full of fairies and unicorns and nice people.'

'Nan, tell me.'

She takes a deep breath, looks around to check no one's coming, then whispers, 'Sue Danalis has baked razorblades into her cake.'

'What?!'

'That's why she entered the competition. She hates Beryl Andrews, one of the judges. Beryl ran off with Sue's ex-husband, so Sue's out for revenge.'

'Really?' I look her in the eye.

'Girl Guides' honour,' she says, holding up three fingers on her right hand. Nan never says 'Girl Guides' honour' unless she's telling the truth. And this definitely sounds like something Jack's nan would do. She once tried to beat my nan up in a back-alley brawl. She almost ran her over in a hot-pink granny cart with monster truck wheels. And, once, I nearly suffocated when Sue farted in my face while she was doing the Downward Dog position in yoga. And, believe me, it was no accident – it was an assassination attempt.

I look up. The edge of the cake plate hangs out from the lip of the window.

I'm stuck. It's wrong to steal. But it's worse to kill. Sue Danalis has turned a fruitcake into a deadly weapon. Is it okay to steal if it stops someone from killing?

Tom Weekly's Guide to Deadly Weapons

Beretta pistol

Ninja star

Sue Danaliss's bottom

Knuckle duster

Flick knife

Grenade

Razorblade fruitcake

'Help me up,' I say, pulling my balaclava over my face again.

'That's my boy,' she says.

Nan knits her hands together. I plant my Converse in the stirrup and push up, half-expecting Nan's hands to break apart, but she's a tough old bird. Those fingers have been working out in the knitting gym since 1963. Her knuckles are glued together. I press myself against the rough brick and reach up until my fingers brush the bottom of the plate.

'Bit higher,' I whisper.

She groans and strains, and I push up on my tippy-toes. Just as I reach for the edge of the plate . . . it disappears. The window slams shut with a *bang*. Nan's hands come apart and I fall, landing on top of her, squishing her into the garden bed.

Nan groans.

'Sorry, Nan.'

'Get off me, you big galoot,' she croaks. 'Have you got the cake?'

'It's gone,' I say.

Sue Danalis revs the engine on her hot-pink motorised granny cart with monster truck wheels. Nan and I are standing at the doorway to the Scout hall where the fruitcakes are about to be judged, and Sue is driving up the wheelchair ramp. She brakes hard and squeals to a stop.

'Hello, Nancy,' she rasps, looking down at us. 'Ready to get knocked off your fruitcake throne?'

'Not likely, fatso,' Nan snaps back.

I nudge Nan. Jack's grandmother is the largest human I've seen outside of the *Guinness World Records*, but it's still mean.

'I'm going to show the people of this town what a *real* fruitcake tastes like,' Sue threatens. 'And teach my enemies a little lesson.'

'You –'

Nan is interrupted by an announcement over the speakers: 'Judging of the fruitcake competition is about to commence. Please make your way to the main hall for the annual Kings Bay Show Fruitcake Bake-Off, the highlight of today's program.'

Sue revs her engine again. 'I'll see you from the top of the winner's podium, you old bag.' She lets out the brake and roars off through the large double doors.

'They'd need a crane to get you up there!' Nan shouts. She screws her program into a ball and throws it at Sue's back, hitting her in the large sweaty patch. Sue doesn't turn around.

Inside, Nan and I take our reserved seats in the front row.

'Last year's winner always gets the royal treatment,' Nan says.

The hall is an old timber building with Scout flags on the walls and a stage at the front end. It's packed with about 200 people – a sea of silver hair with a few shiny bald heads bobbing around.

'What should we do?' I ask Nan.

'Sit tight,' she says, chewing on her thumbnail.

'We can't just sit tight. If there are raz–'

'Attention please, everybody,' says a lady onstage in a frail voice. She's wearing spectacles and a big sticker name tag that says 'Beryl'. 'Thank you for coming to the judging. I'm sure it'll be an event that we'll all remember for a very long time.'

I twist in my seat to see Sue parked at the back of the hall, a shifty look in her eye. Although, Sue always has a shifty look in her eye, so it's difficult to tell if this is shiftier than usual.

Beryl explains the judging criteria: aroma, moistness and flavour. 'And, now for the judges' tasting!' she announces to wild applause. 'Afterwards, there'll be tea and samples of each cake for you to try and select the People's Choice winner.'

Another burst of applause.

Seven fruitcakes are lined up on a long trestle table covered in a pink floral plastic tablecloth. Nan's is first, on the far left. Beryl cuts the cake and passes a small slice on a plate down to each of the other three judges.

The crowd falls silent.

Nan watches, mouth open, eyes flitting from one judge to the next.

They chew carefully, jotting notes on their pads. They gather and mutter to one another.

Oh, the tension . . .

The crowd mutters, too.

The judges mutter some more.

The tension in the room is unbearable with all this muttering. Beryl stands, her chair scraping the floor, calling for silence.

'The judges have decided . . . that Nancy Weekly's cake . . . is . . .'

Nan's brows are narrowed.

'. . . a nine out of ten!' Beryl announces.

There's a big round of applause. I put my arm around Nan. I'm so proud of her. She laughs, raises her hand to say thank you and turns to look over her shoulder at Sue. Nan gives her a *beat that!* kind of a look.

Beryl passes the microphone down the line and the judges use words like, 'Delectable', 'Scrumptious' and 'A revelation!' to describe Nan's cake.

'Now, a first-time entrant in the fruitcake competition – although, she did come *ninth* in the pickled onions category in 2011.'

A wicked smile slithers across Beryl's lips. 'Sue Danalis!'

One person claps up the back. It's Sue. The sound echoes around the hall. I think her fan club has yet to sign its first member.

'That's enough now, thank you, Sue,' Beryl warns, and she begins cutting the cake.

'You have to say something,' I whisper to Nan.

'No. Let her rot in jail.'

'But if –'

'Give her 25 years, for all I care.'

'You can't just –'

'I never really liked Beryl Andrews much anyway,' she says. 'She's a sticky-beak.

And she once accused me of using *imported* sultanas.'

Beryl slices the cake and passes the plates along to the other judges.

I can't believe how heartless my grandmother is being. It makes me feel as though she might be in on this. Are she and Sue partners in crime? Did Beryl try to steal Pop away, too? From where I sit, I can't quite see what they found so irresistible about her.

Beryl hasn't discovered the secret ingredient yet. Sue leans forward on her granny cart, eyes glued to the stage. Her hands clasp the steering wheel tight as Beryl and the other judges delicately raise the cake to their mouths.

'What if she kills all four of them?' I whisper.

Nan presses her lips together. She looks up

to the stage, nervous. She's ready to stand and
say something. But then she doesn't.

I can't take it anymore. If I do nothing,
Nan's cake might win but innocent people
will die. As the cake touches Beryl's lips I leap
to my feet and scream, 'STOP!'

The judges look up, mouths open, forks
frozen in front of their lips. The hall is silent.
Two hundred old, agitated faces stare at me.

'What is it, young man?' Beryl croaks into
the microphone.

I turn to Sue, who scowls and combs her wispy moustache with her fingers.

'There's razorb . . .' I begin.

'Excuse me?' Beryl asks.

I look down at Nan and then I step forward. 'There are razorblades in that cake,' I say in a loud, clear voice.

Everyone in the hall murmurs.

'QUIET, please,' Beryl says into the microphone. 'What do you mean, "razorblades"?'

'Sue Danalis,' I say, pointing at her. 'She put razorblades in the cake.'

There are gasps around the hall.

'I knew she was a bad egg,' a man in the row behind me whispers to his wife. 'A big bad ostrich egg.'

'That's ridiculous!' Beryl says.

'I'll show you,' I tell her.

I climb the small set of stairs.

'Get him off that stage!' Sue calls out.
'He'd better not lay a finger on that fruitcake.'

'The boy's mad,' someone else shouts.

I take Beryl's fork and dig into the cake,
pulling it apart. Sue is granny-cart-speeding
down the side of the hall, knocking into chairs.
'Get your rotten little hands off my cake!'

I work faster, mashing the cake with the
fork, squashing it into the plate to reveal the
razorblades and thwart the evil plan. The cake
is a pile of rubble now. I'm searching through
the crumbs, but I can't see a single razorblade.

'Look what you've done, you silly boy,'
Beryl snips.

I turn to Nan in the front row for an
explanation. Audience members shout some

not-very-nice things at me, like, 'Fruitcake hater!' Nan beckons me with one bony finger. Sue's hot-pink granny cart turns the corner at the front of the hall with a squeal of tyres on polished floorboards.

'Excuse me for one moment,' I say to Beryl.

'This had better be good!' she growls.

I slink off the stage, down the wobbly wooden stairs and over to Nan.

I sit down next to her. 'What happened?'

'Well . . .' she whispers.

'Well what?'

'The thing is . . .'

'Nan!' I warn.

Sue is speeding along the front of the hall towards us. People in the front row pull their feet back to stop their toes being squished by the huge, chunky tyres.

Now, THIS is a scary sight.

'I only told you there were razorblades so you'd help me steal the cake, you dingbat,' Nan whispers.

'What?!'

'I only –'

'I heard what you said! Why would you do that? You said, "Girl Guides' Honour".'

'I was never even *in* the Girl Guides, nitwit,' she snaps.

Sue's cart is almost upon us so I jump to my feet, run in front of it and clamber onto the stage. Nan scuttles away down the aisle to escape.

I grab the microphone from Beryl and clear my throat.

Sue's cart pulls up next to the stairs.

The crowd falls silent. They look like they may want to rip my guts out.

'Um . . . sorry about that,' I say. 'My bad.'

Shouts from the crowd.

Sue lowers her enormous frame down off her cart and mounts the stairs to the stage.

I quickly attempt to mould the pile of crumbs into something that looks a bit like a cake.

'There you go. Good as new,' I say, forcing a smile. I look to Nan for help but she's disappeared.

Sue reaches the top of the stairs, glaring at me, wheezing from the effort.

'You destroyed my cake,' she huffs. 'Now I destroy you.' She grabs my arm but I twist out of her grasp and scurry across the stage in front of the cake table. Just as I go to leap down the stairs, on the far side I hear cries of 'No!' from the audience.

I turn and I'm smacked in the face by a whole fruitcake. It's hard as a brick and knocks me off my feet. The cake lands on the stage with a thud and splits in two. My face tingles. Blood trickles from my nose.

The audience is on their feet now, outraged that Sue has thrown someone else's cake. So I do the natural thing. I get to my feet, pick up a cake from my end of the trestle table and frisbee it at her. It carves through the air and

hits her right in the guts. She doubles over
with an *oof*.

Sue's not down for long. She grabs the
nearest cake, winds up and pitches it at me.
I sidestep and it hits the male judge standing
behind me in the neck, then explodes off the
wall at the side of the stage.

'Right!' he says and snatches up another
cake, pegging it at Sue. It's an amazing shot.
She cops it right in the forehead and the cake
detonates, sending big, brown fruity chunks
flying everywhere.

Only two cakes remain. One of the
bakers, Fay Crabtree, who used to own the
newsagency, storms the stage and seizes her
cake. 'Hands off!' She scampers away, almost
getting hit in the crossfire as Sue picks up the
last cake and hurls it into the crowd, shouting,

'Eat that, haters! I know none of you like me, and I'm glad!'

People jump to their feet, screaming and throwing lumps of cake back at Sue. The room is a zoo.

'Everybody!' Beryl calls into the microphone as a cake nugget flies past. 'Please settle down.'

Sue tries to duck and weave the cake bombs but she's not that nimble. She leans forward and overbalances. She swings her arms in circles, trying to hang onto the air, but air has no handles. She howls as she topples from the stage. There's a lady and man standing on the floor below her. It's Fay Crabtree and her husband, gently placing the last remaining cake into a Tupperware container. They look up and raise their arms, trying to protect themselves from the wrecking ball, but it's no good. Sue lands on top of Fay, her husband and the last surviving cake, squishing all three of them into the floor.

At the back of the hall, the shadowy figure of Nancy Weekly slips out into the sunshine.

Fay Crabtree is awarded an honorary first prize for the fruitcake bake-off, even though her entry was more like a pancake when they peeled it off the floor. The judges thought the prize might speed her and her husband's recovery down at Kings Bay Memorial Hospital.

The president of the Kings Bay Show gives me two weeks of afternoon community work at the Scout hall to 'think about what I've done'. Packing up chairs and tables, sweeping and wiping, painting, cleaning toilets. It stinks.

I don't speak to Nan during that time. I'm pretty angry with her. I figure I'll give her some time to think about what *she's* done. On my final afternoon of community service, I drop by her place to give her a piece of my mind. Someone has to tell her that she can't just go around stealing and lying and cheating people. As I head around the back of her house I start to get cold feet. I guess I don't want to be too hard on her. She must feel pretty bad after everything that's happened.

I find her in the kitchen, blinds drawn, hunched over the dining table.

'What are you doing?'

'Studying,' she says.

'Studying what?'

'A map.'

'A map of what?'

'The nursing home. I think our mistake was waiting till the cake was on the window sill. Next year, we'll break in and steal it right out of the oven.'

What Would You Rather Do?

* Have a zombie eat your brain or a werewolf eat your heart?

* Be invisible or twice as tall as the current tallest human?

* Be eaten alive by leeches or mosquitoes?

* Eat a whole black pudding (a sausage made from pig's blood) or be a pig for a month?

* Have your earlobe caught by a fish hook or every hair on your head pulled out one by one?

* Only eat lollies or pizza for the rest of your life?

* Lie on a bed of nails or be fired from a cannon?

* Get a tattoo of an emu on your forehead or a tattoo of your worst enemy on your bum?

* Be the fastest kid in your class or the strongest?

* Abseil down the side of a skyscraper or dive off a tall bridge?

* Have no school holidays for an entire year or do only your worst subject for a term?

* Read 100 very long chapter books in the next year or eat one book now?

* Be a world-champion nosepicker or the worst player in the world at your favourite sport?

* Have a boxing match with an angry kangaroo (an angaroo) or do the splits on an echidna?

* Listen to classical music for a week or a non-stop fart for 24 hours straight?

* Eat a swimming pool full of jelly in one sitting or a bowl full of llama spit?

Detention

'I'm gonna get you, Weekly. This is your fault,'
Brent Bunder croaks, pointing one of his big,
fat sausage fingers at me. I don't like it much
when Brent points his sausage fingers at me.
Besides, it's not my fault at all. Brent chucked
the pear and broke the window, not me.

'I shall be next door in the staff room
attending an important meeting,' says
Mr Skroop. He's standing at the front of
the classroom. Skroop is a beanstalk of a
man and has a long nose with hairs sticking

out of it. Our projects on 'Crime and Punishment' are on the wall behind him. We've been studying the legal system and thinking about what should happen to people who break the law. I'm not a fan of Skroop's brand of punishment at all.

BeaN   Beanstalk

'If any of you move, speak or breathe too heavily I will know about it and you will all be back for lunchtime detention tomorrow. Do I make myself clear?'

We all nod. No one has admitted to smashing Skroop's office window with the pear, so the whole class has been given detention. Everybody knows it was Brent but they're too scared to say, on account of him being four times the size of a normal human child. And the fact that he could snap us in two with his big toe if he wanted to.

'I can't hear you,' Skroop says, a hand cupped to his ear.

'YES, MISTER SKROOP!' we all say, trying to deafen him. I was, anyway.

He strides to the door. I swear he says 'imbeciles' under his breath. I didn't know

what an imbecile was till I met Mr Skroop.
Now I've been called an imbecile at least 45
times, as well as 'twit', 'delinquent' and 'idiot'.
Not that I'm counting.

Skroop leaves the door open and slithers
up the hall.

Sasha knows I was involved in the Pear
Incident and she gives me a filthy look, which
jabs me in the heart. I'm pretty young to
have found the woman I'm going to marry
but, when you find the one, you just know.
Sasha and I are going to have three kids and a
labradoodle and a house overlooking the ocean
with secret passages and revolving bookcases.
I haven't mentioned this to Sasha yet. I'm
waiting for the right time. Probably not now.

'Who wants to have some fun?' Jack says,
getting up from his seat.

'Sit down, Jack,' Sasha warns.

'Skroop won't come back,' Jack says. 'Relax. Teachers just say all that "Don't speak. Don't breathe" stuff to make you think they know everything.'

Jack goes to the whiteboard on wheels at the front of the room. He starts to draw a picture, beginning with a long nose that looks suspiciously like Mr Skroop's. He draws long hairs sprouting from it and gets a few laughs.

'*What* do you think you are doing?' says a voice from the doorway.

It's Mr Skroop.

Jack gulps.

'Lunchtime detention for all of you, tomorrow,' he says.

'Good one, Jack!' Brent hisses and throws a pen at him.

'Who threw that?' Skroop demands. 'Who threw that missile?'

Brent puts up his hand. Finally, he's admitting to something.

'It was Weekly, sir,' Brent says.

'*What*?' I spit.

'That's another detention on Wednesday,' Skroop announces. 'We're going to have some very sad, very hungry children by the end of the week, aren't we, Weekly?' He glares at me and heads off down the hall again.

No one says a word but the whole room stinks of dirty looks. Most of the stench is aimed at me.

I feel a tap on my shoulder. I turn to see that Stella Holling has dropped a note down the back of my seat. She flutters her eyelashes.

Stella
Holling
is a
Vampire!

I choose to ignore it. Stella Holling is always passing me notes and fluttering her eyelashes. When will she get the message? This boat has floated. This plane has flown. This train has left the station. Sasha and I are a sure thing. Just as soon as I get up the courage to ask Jack to ask Sasha's friend Sophie if she thinks that Sasha will go out with me again.

After a minute I'm bored, and I'm also worried that someone else might snatch Stella's note and read it out to the class, so I reach around and grab it. It's on pink paper and stinks of perfume.

Jack leans in to read it with me.

Dear Wolfy, it begins. She's taken to calling me Wolfy since the school performance of Little Red Riding Hood, where I played Mr Wolf and she tried to trick me into kissing her in front of the entire school.

Dear Wolfy. I believe you when you say that you didn't throw the pear. And I saw Brent throw the pen. Please turn around once you've read this. Kiss-kiss. Your future wife, Stella.

Jack laughs. 'I bags being best man.'

I ball the letter up in my fist. The palm of my hand is stained with Stella's perfume.

It smells like rotten strawberries and vinegar. I turn slowly, my eyes rolled so far up into their sockets that they might slip over into the back of my skull.

Stella launches herself forward and smacks a kiss right on my lips in front of everyone.

'Oooooooooo!' half the class choruses. 'Shhhhhhhh!' the other half whisper.

Within seconds Skroop is at the door.

'Detention!' he snaps. 'Thursday. What was that ruckus about?'

I wipe my lips on the collar of my school shirt.

'Tell me now. What was that disturbance about?'

I silently pray that no one will tell him that Stella kissed me.

'Weekly kissed Holling, sir,' Brent offers.

'That's a lie!' I explode.

'Did too. Look, you can see her pink lip stuff on his collar.'

I look down. It's true. My white collar is smeared with 'pink lip stuff'.

'Another detention for you all!' Skroop shouts. 'There will be no kissing in my classroom, Weekly, do you understand?'

Sasha glares at me. I hang my head in shame. I'm going to need a lip replacement before the wedding day.

I want to tell Skroop that Stella hurled herself at me, that I'm irresistible to her – the Weekly Vibe is just too strong. But if I've learned one thing about Walton Skroop, it's that it's better to say nothing.

'Yes, Mister Skroop.'

'If I have to leave my meeting to come back into this room one more time, it's detention for the rest of the term for all of you! Are we clear?'

'Yes, Mis-ter Skroop,' we all groan.

He slides out of the room again.

'Hey, girls,' Brent whispers. I turn and he's looking directly at me and Jack. 'Wanna play catch?' He holds up an old brown pear. Is he kidding? Does he have a pear farm in his bag?

'Don't you dare, Brent,' Sasha says. 'That's what got us into this trouble in the first place.'

'Are you saying I done it?' Brent asks.

'*Everyone* knows you *did* it,' Sasha snaps.

Sasha's braver than I am. Brent's a scary guy. He once tried to stuff me in the rubbish bin . . . the one under the teacher's desk.

'If Weekly hadn't ducked, that pear would have hit him in the head instead of smashin' Skroop's window. So it's *his* fault.'

Jonah, Brent's snivelling best friend, laughs a blocked-nose snort that turns into a cough.

'Here's a little present for you, Weekly.' Brent hurls the pear across the classroom at me. I can't believe this is happening for the second time today. I'm a pear magnet. Pears love me. They are the Stella Hollings of the fruit world.

Reading Brent Bunder's mind is actually pretty easy...

Kill. Weekly.

It's sailing towards my head. I'm ducking but it's still coming. There's no way I'll get lucky a second time – but I do. *WHOOM*. It soars past my ear and hits the wheelie whiteboard, exploding on impact. It spatters the Crime and Punishment projects. The judge in the middle of mine is now wearing a pear-covered wig. It's all over the teacher's desk, on the carpet, everywhere.

We all sit up straight, listen and wait for Skroop, knowing that the end is nigh.

No footsteps.

No shout of, 'Detention!'

We wait for thirty seconds, a minute.

Still nothing.

I turn to Brent, who's smiling his broken-toothed smile. I see how angry Sasha and a bunch of the others are with what he's done.

We're going to be ready to retire before this detention ends.

I decide that I've had enough of being blamed and scared and pushed around by this oversized toddler with facial hair. I'm tired of him ruling our year. If Sasha can stand up to him, I can too. I go to the board and start scraping together the spattered pear.

'Don't, Tom,' a few kids say, Sasha among them.

I continue to scrape. I can think of three good reasons not to do what I'm about to do with the remains of this pear:

1) Skroop

2) Sasha

3) Brent.

But I don't care. It was Brent who broke the window and blamed it on me, Brent who threw the pen and blamed it on me, Brent who told everyone that *I'd* kissed *Stella*. And now this.

I can hear Brent mouth-breathing up the back of the room. I can smell his fishy aroma. And I know it's time. I pat together a roughly pear-sized ball of fruity goo and turn to my nemesis.

'You better not be doin' what I think yer doin', Weekly,' Brent says.

I rear my hand back, ready to throw. A gentle grin washes over my face. Goo drips from between my fingers and onto the floor. Every other kid between me and Brent hides beneath their desk.

'If you throw that, Weekly, I'm gonna flatten you like a . . . piece of toast, y'hear me?'

'No,' I say. 'I don't hear you. This is for everything you've done to all of us.'

And I throw.

'Weekly, *what* is going on?!' says Skroop from the doorway. But it's too late. The pear mush has left my hand and is soaring across the room. It holds together pretty well until about halfway. Then it starts to break apart and there are suddenly three, then nine, then eighty-one pear missiles heading towards Brent Bunder.

Brent screams, 'Weeeekly!'

Schloomp.

It hits him in the face, the hair, the ears, the neck, chest, shoulders, arms and belly. He's polka-dotted with rotten pear slop.

The whole class starts to laugh from under their desks. They can't help it. Jack, Sasha, Stella, Lewis, Jonah – everyone is falling about. Even Skroop stifles a laugh.

slow motion detention generator

The only people in the room not laughing are me and Brent.

'Detention for the rest of the term for Bunder and Weekly. The rest of you are dismissed.'

The other kids clear out within seconds.

'This will be a very, very long term for you, gentlemen. You can begin by cleaning up this mess.'

Brent glares at me, his eyes boring tiny holes in my soul as he wipes splodges of brown goop from his face.

'NOW!' Skroop shouts and Bunder starts moving towards me at the front of the room. I back up. He's gathering speed, running at me now. Desks and chairs fly to the side as he rushes down the aisle.

'Brent!' Skroop warns.

But Brent doesn't listen. He's a raging bull charging at the red cape of my face. I'm frozen to the spot. He's going to tackle me through the wall and into the next room if I don't move. At the last second, I duck to my left. Bunder's forehead and right fist go through the wheelie whiteboard with an almighty *crunch*.

Skroop and I look on, shocked. We can only see Brent from the neck down. His head has disappeared through the board. He pulls his fist out and tries to pull his head out but he's too stunned and groggy. He growls in pain. Brent turns, the board wheeling around with him, until he's facing me and Skroop. He looks like a convict.

'I'm gonna get you, Weekly,' he says.

'No, you're not. You've already missed me with two pears.'

This is a new look for Brent Bunder and I like it!

'The first one missed you by half a millimetre, and the second one –' Brent stops and glances nervously at Skroop. He tries to smile, knowing he's dropped himself in it.

'Bunder, thank you very much. I suspected you were the culprit. Detention for the rest of the term! Weekly, dismissed.'

The lunch bell goes. I grab my essay on Crime and Punishment sticky-taped dangerously close to Bunder's face. He tries to bite my hand, but I'm too quick. I skip off out the door and, for once in my life, justice has been served.

I'VE DECIDED TO
EAT A CAR

I've decided to eat a car.

I need to make my mark on the world,

to be remembered.

Humans have climbed Mt Everest,

flown to the moon,

grown eyebrow hairs 19 centimetres long.

But how does a primary school kid

get the attention and respect he deserves

in this world?

I'll tell you how.

He eats a car.

I guess I could do something else.

A walk for charity.

Find the cure for a disease.

Or work out, once and for all,

why weekends are two days,

and the school week is five.

But eating a car is more my style.

It's original. Fresh.

I mean, how many people

do you know

who have eaten a vehicle?

Probably none.

I might have a plane for dessert.

I'll be like Michel Lotito,

the Frenchman they call Monsieur Mangetout –

'Mr Eats All'.

He ate 18 bikes,

a pair of snow skis,

and an aeroplane.

But never a car.

No one has ever eaten a car.

Yet.

I figure I'll clean the car out first in case
there's Lego stuck between the seats.
That stuff can really hurt.
For entree, I could eat all the chips and
biscuits and mixed nuts
I find down in the cracks.

Mixed nuts and bolts

Then I'll eat the baby wipes

and maps and manuals

in the glovebox.

Then the car mats and carpet,

which will tickle my throat,

the seat covers and tyres, quite chewy.

I wonder what a door would taste like.

And for main course? The engine.

Smothered in custard and ice-cream.

It's 5.36 on a Wednesday afternoon.

I walk into the lounge room.

Mum's sitting on the couch, staring at her phone.

I tell her that I'm going to eat a car.

You know what she says?

'That's nice, mate.'

She doesn't even look up.

Can you believe that?

Her only son is about to devour

a rear-vision mirror,

a car stereo,

and an exhaust pipe,

and she says, 'That's nice.'

'Are you listening to me?' I ask.

'*Mm-hmm*,' she says in that vague, distant way

that parents say things. 'Have fun.'

Now I'm annoyed.

She isn't taking me seriously.

'I might eat *your* car,' I tell her.

'That's good,' she says, pressing send on her

text and opening up mail.

'Alrighty then. I'm off to eat the car.'

'Do whatever you like. Just give me five

minutes' peace.'

And that seals the deal.

I'm actually going to do it.

I was kind of kidding before,

but now I'm sure.

This might be the only way

I can get my mother and the world

to sit up and take notice of me.

I step inside the dark garage and flick

on the light.

I stare at the car –

at its hard, red surfaces,

with patches of rust.

When Mum comes out in the morning,

ready to drive to work,

and the garage is empty,

she'll scream, 'Somebody's stolen the car!'

I'll just burp

and casually pick metal scraps from my teeth.

I'm glad it's only a hatchback.

For the first time in my life,

I'm happy that my mum doesn't drive

a stretch limo.

I open the back door on the passenger side.

The first thing I see

is a whole bunch of sultanas

down the edge of the seat.

I think I remember dropping them there

when I was three.

I pick one up,

dust the sand off.

It looks hard

and dry

and mean.

I put it in my mouth.

I chew.

And chew.

I swallow.

Not too bad for food that's eight years old.
I poke my finger down
and pick up another sultana.
I eat that, too.
By the time I've eaten
all the dried fruit and almonds and
rice cracker crumbs from between the seats
I'm almost full.
I can barely even look at the car manual
and maps and wipes.
But I've made a promise to myself.
A man's gotta do what a man's gotta do.
Serves Mum right for ignoring me.
Serves the *world* right for ignoring me.
They'll all wish they'd been nicer.
They'll be desperate to hear what I've got to say
when I'm on the *Today Show*,
giving my top five tips on how to eat a car.

I slide into the driver's seat.

I lean forward

and sink my teeth into the steering wheel.

It's leathery and delicious. Like a steak,

sort of.

Best steering wheel I've ever tasted.

The Angriest Ice-Cream Man in Australia

Our new ice-cream man is the angriest ice-cream man in Australia. I think he's forgotten what it's like to be a kid.

'Should I have strawberry whipple, Lemony Snicket or peppermint crunch?' I ask.

It's one of the hottest days of summer, and Jack and I are standing at the wide window on the side of the pink ice-cream truck. 'Greensleeves' is playing on never-ending repeat through the loudspeaker on top of the van. The ice-cream man is tall with a crisp white shirt and very neat hair. He's sweating like crazy.

'I honestly don't care,' he snaps, which hurts my feelings a bit. Pearl, the old ice-cream lady, was really nice. She used to give us tall towers of vanilla goodness, with free chocolate sprinkles. I think that's why she went out of business. Sprinkles can really add up.

'But which would *you* choose?' I ask.

'None of them.'

'If it was life or death?' Jack asks.

'Under what circumstances would eating ice-cream be "life or death"?' he asks. 'And I don't eat ice-cream.'

Jack and I look at each other, gobsmacked.

'You're an ice-cream man and you don't eat ice-cream?' I ask.

'Ice-cream is for babies and spoilt brats. Now, what do you want? You're wasting my time. I have other customers.'

I turn around. The street is empty apart from the blind, three-legged dog with the broken tail from number 47, who is licking an old, flattened cane toad in the middle of the road.

'One whipple, one crunch,' Jack says. 'And make 'em big.'

The IceCreaminator zaps Jack with spinning strawberry whipple eyes of death.

'Please?' Jack asks.

The man starts to make the ice-creams, banging things around and muttering under his breath. I start to worry he might poison my whipple. I watch him carefully.

'Sixteen bucks,' he announces, placing two very small cones with two minuscule

scoops in the holder on the counter in front
of us.

'Sixteen dollars?!' Jack spits.

'Did I stutter?' He slides out a hand with
unnecessarily long fingers.

'But it's only two ice-creams,' Jack says.
'We don't want to buy the whole truck!'

'Eight dollars each.'

'But a kids' cone is usually two dollars.
Look, it says so on the sign.' Jack points.

The ice-cream man rips the cardboard sign
off the counter, tears it in half and drops it on
the floor. 'New owner. New prices. New ice-
cream. It's a better product – gluten-free and
organic.'

'We don't want gluten-free and organic!'
I tell him. 'Why would you try to turn ice-
cream into a health food? That defeats the

whole purpose of eating it. We want the cheapest, nastiest stuff you've got, so long as it's cold, in a cone and costs us less than four bucks for two, 'cause that's all we have.'

'Oh, well. What a shame. No ice-cream for you.' He snatches the cones from the holder and drops them into a bin with a *clang*.

'What're you *doing*?' Jack asks.

The ice-cream man slams down the metal roller shutter on the side of his van. I hear a lock slide across and three quick footsteps inside. The engine roars, there's a squeal of tyres, and the van takes off, almost running over my foot and only narrowly missing the blind dog with the broken tail.

Jack and I stand in the middle of the street, open-mouthed, sun-sweltered and ice-cream-less. Even the dog looks shocked as the little pink van turns the corner and disappears in a cloud of exhaust and warbling 'Greensleeves'.

'Can you believe that?' I say. 'He threw perfectly good ice-cream in the bin.'

'He's gonna pay.'

'How?'

'We'll hold up the van and steal all his ice-cream,' Jack suggests. 'Next Saturday we hide and, when he stops, we'll stick him up like bushrangers. We'll be stealing from the rich and giving to the sugar-deprived.'

'Isn't that kind of illegal?' I ask.

'Isn't it kind of illegal for a guy with a van loaded with delicious, creamy treats to go *parading* through the streets charging prices that normal people can't afford? I mean, which is worse?'

I think about it for a second. 'Probably still the holding-up-the-truck thing.'

'We'll take every tub,' Jack says. 'Choc-chip, Snickers, caramel swirl –'

'Or we could just start our own ice-cream stand?' I suggest.

... but we still got:
Choc-chip Brussels Sprout,
Boot polish Crunch,
Eggplant ripple and
Dog poo swirl.
That last one's
my favourite!

ICE CREAM

Next Saturday afternoon, Jack and I are sitting at a fold-up table on the kerb in front of my place. It's even hotter than last week. Thirty-six degrees, they reckon.

'Two dollars, please,' I say.

Nick Crabtree flips me a coin, takes his ice-cream and walks away past the other 12 or 13 kids and parents in line. Nick's little sister Elsie steps up to the table.

'Pink, white or brown?' Jack asks.

'Pink, please,' she says.

Jack digs his soup spoon into the eight-litre container of store-brand Neapolitan ice-cream, jams a gigantic scoop into a cone and hands it over. It's the cheapest ice-cream you can get, and it's been in the freezer in our garage since the last ice age. When we pried open the lid we had to dig out half a kilo of ice crystals. Our policy is: 'What the customer doesn't know won't kill them.'

Elsie smiles, slides her coin across the table, and I drop it into a Ziploc bag with the 30 or so bucks we've made in the last hour. This is our best get-rich-quick scheme since we sold head lice in the school playground.

'Pink, white or brown?' Jack asks. I pass him a fresh cone – well, fresh-ish. The cones have been in the top of Jack's pantry for a couple of summers. There are a few bite marks on some of the cones where mice have nibbled through the box, but they're still remarkably crisp. They're from a jumbo pack of 80, made from pure, sweet gluten.

Then I hear the haunting sound of 'Greensleeves' in the distance.

'Here we go.'

'You ready?' Jack asks.

'I guess.'

The van tears around the corner of my street with a howl of tyres. I swear the ice-cream man is driving so fast he gets it up on two wheels.

He speeds up the hill towards us and sees Jack and me sitting on the kerb with a queue of customers. He slams on the brakes, scattering the customers at the front of the line, and the van screeches to a stop right next to our table. He rolls down the front passenger window and rips off a pair of dark sunglasses.

'What do you two dummies think you're doing?'

'Selling ice-cream,' Jack says with a grin. 'Would you like one? Two dollars. Please pull your vehicle around to the drive-through window.'

The ice-cream man kills the engine, pops the door of the van and climbs down.

'You can't sell ice-cream in the street!' he tells us. 'It's illegal.'

'You do it,' Jack says.

'I have a licence.'

'Well,' Jack says, 'we don't. *Next*!'

'A comb wiv sprinkles,' says Jet, a five-year-old kid from the house on the corner. I take Jet's money, sprinkle hundreds and thousands on his ice-cream and hand him the cone.

The ice-cream man looms over us like a dark cloud. The next customers in line look a bit scared.

Surely <u>THE</u> best licence in the entire world !

ICE-CREAM LICENCE

Card no: 2694   Tom Weekly

Licence no:
6794402M

'Shut this operation down right now!' he threatens. His very neat hair trembles with rage.

Jack slams down his spoon and stands, his chair scraping across the gravel on the edge of the road. I know better than anyone when Jack has had enough.

'You listen here, angry ice-cream man. How about you go and get into your little pink truck and try selling one of your health-food ice-creams someplace else – this is our turf now. Go on! Scram!'

'Scwam!' says a two-year-old who's sitting up on his dad's shoulders at the front of the line.

'Give the kids a break, mate,' the dad says. 'They're being entrepreneurial.'

The ice-cream man growls, twists around and heads for his truck. 'You'll pay for this!'

'Maybe, but we won't pay eight bucks!' Jack yells.

The man gets in, speed-reverses his van to the other side of the street and shouts, 'I'm calling the police!' He dials and puts the phone to the side of his beet-red face. I'm worried his head might explode from the heat. It sure must be hot up in that little truck.

Jack and I work double-time, trying to serve everyone in line before the cops show up and shut us down.

When we're done I drop the last two dollars into the Ziploc bag, Jack folds up the table, and I look over to the ice-cream man. He's sitting at the wide window on the side of his truck. For some reason I feel kind of bad for him. I wander over and he scowls. He wipes the sweat flooding into his eyes with a dirty blue tea towel.

I reach up and place our last ice-cream in his fancy cone holder.

He stares at it, then looks at me.

'Try it,' I say.

'I told you. I don't like ice-cream. It's for babies and spoilt brats.'

'That's not true,' I say. 'Everyone likes ice-cream.'

'Not me.' He fans his face with a piece of the torn-up price list. 'Where are the cops?'

'Go on,' I say. 'It'll cool you down. I managed to get all three flavours in one scoop.'

I'm concerned his head might burst into flames if he doesn't eat it. He eyes the ice-cream, swallows hard, frowns at me. He reaches out, picks up the cone. He inspects it, sneers, pokes his tongue out and makes contact with the ice-cream.

I watch his eyes as the sweet, cold, creamy goodness hugs his tastebuds.

He takes a bite.

I hear a single note from a siren as a police car pulls up behind the van. It's Sergeant John

Hategarden at the wheel. Jack and I have had a few encounters with Hategarden. Like the time we were attacked by giant mutant head lice. And when I accidentally crashed Nan's car into the Kings Bay public swimming pool.

The policeman climbs out of his car and puts on his hat as the ice-cream man takes another big bite. I can tell he likes it. Hategarden sidles up next to me at the window.

'Can I help you?' he asks.

The ice-cream man wipes his mouth and looks at me, then over at Jack across the street.

'We've had a complaint about an illegal ice-cream operation,' Hategarden says. He doesn't look too impressed to have been called out in the heat. He wipes the river of sweat from the back of his neck.

'Yes . . .' says the ice-cream man.

This is a nightmare. We'll probably have to give the money back. I should have saved the last ice-cream for Hategarden, although bribing a police officer probably wouldn't help our case.

'The problem . . .' says the ice-cream man. His face has faded from a violent crimson to a quieter sort of piglet pink. ' . . . has been fixed.'

Huh?

Hategarden looks at me, then up at the ice-cream man. Ice-cream man winks at me. Hategarden looks relieved. 'Good,' he says. 'Well, I might have an ice-cream.' He takes out his wallet. 'I like the look of the strawberry whipple, the Lemony Snicket and the pepper-mint crunch. Which do you recommend?'

I grin. The ice-cream man and I share a look. I wait for him to say, *I honestly don't care which flavour you choose.* But, instead, he says, 'My customers seem to like the Lemony Snicket.' He starts scooping.

Hategarden gets out a $20 note but the ice-cream man says, 'It's on the house, officer. And how about a free ice-cream for the young man here?'

I grin and nod.

'Might even have another one myself,' he says then laughs – a proper, hearty ice-cream man laugh. 'There we go. Lemony Snicket. And what about you? Strawberry whipple?'

So I eat my first gluten-free, organic ice-cream. It's pretty good, in spite of its health-food properties – a bit of a cross between cardboard and glue, but remarkably refreshing.

From that day on, the ice-cream man switches back to the old ice-cream, and he only ever charges kids two dollars a cone.

Except for me and Jack.

For us, it's free.

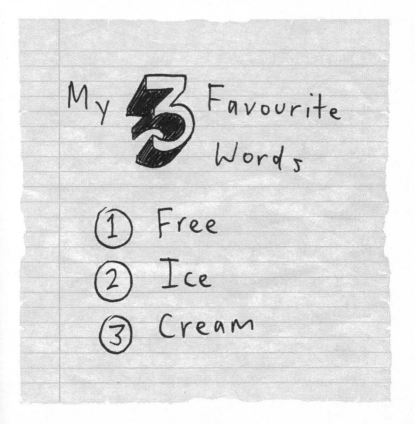

My **3** Favourite Words

(1) Free

(2) Ice

(3) Cream

ButtMan

I have a problem with my bum.

And my mum.

A massive one. (The problem is massive, not my mum or my bum.)

Mum wants to take my bum to the doctor. She says it makes 'unpleasant odours on a far too regular basis'.

But I disagree. I think its odours are quite pleasant. If there was a perfect volume of stink to be discharged from a kid's bottom in a day, mine would come pretty close to

If Mum had her way, I'd be bum-less. (I'd be the butt of everyone's jokes.)

that number. The bum is the most under-appreciated part of the human body. Our bums are always there, supporting us, and we should be kinder to them.

They're comfy to sit on, they keep our pants up and always have our backs. Last weekend, mine won me a farting competition against Jack. I was the underdog going in, but my butt really pulled through for me. Extraordinary muscle control, perfect pitch, not a drop spilt.

When I was seven years old Mum hit me on the bum with an old wooden spoon and it broke in half. (The spoon, not my bum. My bum is already in half.) My butt is a total ninja. It could crack 30 walnuts in 30 seconds. (If I ever need a bunch of walnuts in a hurry.)

Anyway, Mum thinks my bum stinks and she's hidden the tins of baked beans and sauerkraut.

And the sultanas, figs and dried apples.

I have nothing to put on my cereal.

All because of my bum.

Stupid bum.

I'd donate it to science if I didn't think science would donate it back.

Maybe I do need to take it to a doctor. If I didn't like sitting down so much I might have it removed.

The doctor will say, 'What'll it be?'

'Take it all off,' I'll tell him.

'All what?'

'My butt, bozo. And make it snappy.'

'But I am not experienced in buttock removal procedures,' the doctor will reply.

'Listen, I didn't come all the way across town to be told that my bottom can't be removed. It's been nothing but trouble since the day I was born – stinkin' up the nappy, making Mum unhappy. It didn't even photograph well in her bathtub pics. Either you take it off or I take my business elsewhere.'

If that doesn't work out I wonder if I can find a way to freshen things up down there without having my bum lopped off. Maybe I'll invent a personal air-freshening device to hang behind the offending orifice. When the foul air is released it will immediately be cleansed and made to smell like daffodils or petunias or something.

Unpleasant odours? Ghastly scents? Stubborn smells that just won't budge? Try the ButtFresh. Freshens trouser coughs in an instant!

I'll sell millions of them to mothers who have issues with their kids' backsides. And they'll be the world's most popular Father's Day gift – Dads always burp out the wrong end when they're asleep in front of the telly. They'll hand them to girls before their interviews for posh private schools. Orchestra conductors and musicians will wear the ButtFresh under their tuxedoes to avoid those unexpected bum notes. They'll be required wearing in all elevators.

In fact, the ButtFresh could save the world from imminent destruction, depending on how fast it can be adapted for cows. If the BF could convert all that dangerous methane released from cows' bottoms into wonderful, life-giving oxygen, we could reverse global warming.

And then my mum will truly appreciate my talents.

She will think I am a genius.

They will call me ButtMan and put my face on the product's packaging.

I will win the Nobel Prize in Chemistry for solving one of the world's most pant-pressing problems. And when I accept the prize I will thank my mum.

And my bum.

Having a smelly bottom could be the best thing that's ever happened to me.

I am ButtMan, and I'm here to save the world.

EIGHT REASONS TO GET YOUR PARENTS OFF SOCIAL MEDIA. RIGHT. NOW.

1. Next time you get double-bounced off the trampoline and break your arm, your dad might come and help you *before* he posts the video on Facebook.

2. Everybody you know has seen a picture of you doing your first poo on the potty when you were a baby, and it could be why your mum's friends look at you funny. That . . . and all the pics of your adorable little tushy.

3. You'll be able to eat your dinner as soon as you sit down, rather than wait ten minutes till your mum has photographed her masterpiece and it's gone cold.

4. Your dad'll stop posting embarrassing selfies with your teacher in front of your macaroni sculpture at parent–teacher night.

5. Your mum is 'friends' with the mother of your school crush, and she just posted a 'Throwback Thursday' pic of you when you were five, playing UNO in Bob the Builder underpants.

6. Your mum stays up late social media-ing, which makes her tired, which is why her eyeballs just melted.

7. You know that time your sister dressed you up in a feather boa, high heels and lipstick when you were six? Yeah, your boss will find that when you apply for your first job.

8. Your dad might stop trying to go viral with the video of his Man Bra invention.

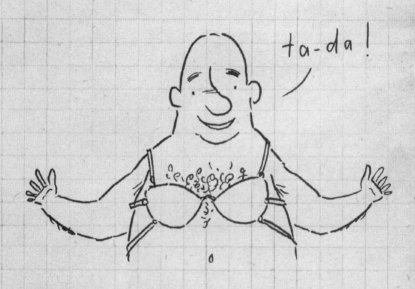

ta-da!

The Wrestler

'Bye-bye, Mummy. Bye, Daddy. Barney wubs
you!'

Jack's mum gives Barney, Jack's four-year-
old brother, a big hug.

'And Mummy wubs you!'

They rub noses and Barney giggles. 'You're
funny, Mummy.'

I'm glad he's happy. It's Jack's parents'
anniversary, so Jack and I are babysitting
him and he can be a bit of a handful. We're
gathered at the front door of the house.

Mr Danalis grabs his jacket. Mrs Danalis glares at me and Jack.

'Are you sure you're up for this?'

'We're sure,' Jack says.

'You won't be mean to him?'

'We won't be mean to him.'

'You'll play games with him?'

'We'll play games with him.'

'You won't wrestle him?'

'We won't wrestle him.'

'Do you remember what happened last time you were trusted with babysitting beautiful Barney?'

'He's not beautiful,' Jack says. 'And, yes, Mum. I rememb–'

'You terrified the poor child and were kicked out of KidsWorld. You and Tom are the only people to have ever been given a lifetime ban.'

'Pretty cool, huh?' Jack says, grinning.

'No, it's not cool.'

'I think you might be forgetting the fact that *he* vomited on *me*,' Jack says, 'and then he had an army of toddlers throw poopy nappies at us.'

'Please don't go into that again, Jack. If you can be beaten up by a gang of babies then perhaps you need to go to the gym and forget about the twenty dollar babysitting fee.'

Jack clenches his jaw. We've already planned what we're spending every cent of that twenty dollars on: Mars bars.

'We'll be fine,' Jack says. 'It's two hours and we're at home in the middle of a rainy day. What could possibly go wrong?'

Mrs D sneers at me and Jack. 'Okay. Well . . . you've got my number –'

Barney

How his parents see him

The truth

'*Nothing* will go wrong.'

'Have fun,' Mr D says in a menacing way, as though he might remove parts of our bodies if we mess this up. Mr D suffers from CDS, Cranky Dad Syndrome. Even when he's being nice he's the scariest person I've ever met.

'But not too much fun,' says Mrs D.

'Enjoy your lunch,' Jack says, pushing them out the front door.

Mrs D puts up an umbrella and they scurry down the puddly path to Mr D's ute. Jack, Barney and I watch from the window, our breath fogging up the glass. Barney waves. Mrs D blows him a kiss as the ute reverses down the driveway and heads off up the street.

The second they disappear from view, Barney turns to me and Jack and wiggles his eyebrows. 'Barney wants to wrestle.'

Barney *always* wants to wrestle. It's his favourite thing in the world. Apart from Milo and cheese sandwiches, slapping people on the back of the neck and picking his nose.

'No, Barney. We can't. We promised Mum,' Jack says. 'Let's play UNO.'

'UNO's poo-poo,' Barney says.

'UNO's not "poo-poo", Barney,' Jack tells him.

'Monopoly?' I suggest.

'Monopoly's bum-bum,' Barney says. 'Barney wanna wrestle.'

'Don't say "bum-bum", Barney,' Jack says.

'*You* just said it!' Barney laughs, pointing right in Jack's face. Then he chants, 'Bum-bum Bar-ney. Bum-bum Bar-ney!'

'We can't wrestle today,' Jack says. 'You got a concussion last time.'

'I promise not to get percussion again,' he says. 'Pleeeeeease.'

The thing is, when Barney gets the idea of wrestling in his head it's almost impossible to talk him out of it.

'If you get hurt or something gets broken, we miss out on twenty bucks.'

'I'll give you twenny bucks!' Barney says, and he races off down the hall.

He's back a moment later with a twenty cent coin. He hands it to Jack with a big gap-toothed grin.

Jack rolls his eyes. He can't even be bothered explaining.

'Pleeeeeease,' Barney says. 'If you do, you'll be the bestest big brother in the whole wide world *ever*.'

Jack likes the sound of this. I don't think he's ever been bestest at anything in his whole life. He looks at me. I shrug, even though alarm bells are ringing like crazy in my head.

'Alright,' Jack says. 'But only for ten minutes.'

'YES!' Barney cheers and races off down the hall again.

'But if you get hurt and we get in trouble, I'm gonna give you an atomic wedgie so big they'll have to operate to remove it,' Jack calls.

'Deal!' Barney shouts from his room. 'I love eating wedgies. And chippies!'

Moments later he races back towards us wearing a fake black beard, a Batman mask and a tracksuit with a pair of bright red undies over the top. 'Bonesaw's readyyyyyy!' he calls.

That's his wrestling name: Bonesaw. He stole it from one of the Spider-Man movies. He jumps up on the couch, flexes his muscles and kisses each skinny little bicep.

'First,' Jack says, 'we have to move the coffee table and lay down a few rule–'

Barney launches himself off the couch and lands a sharp elbow on Jack's nose.

'Boom!' Barney screams. 'Bonesaw smash!'

BONE SAW!
(more like 'Bone head')

Jack clutches his nose and blood drips from
his left nostril. He shoves Barney back onto
the couch.

'Ow! We haven't even started yet!' Jack yells.

Barney stands and blows kisses to an
imaginary crowd. 'In the blue corner, it's –'

Jack sweeps Barney's legs out from under
him and Barney collapses onto the couch,

laughing, then he leaps to his feet and runs across the room. He acts like he's springing off the ropes on the far side of a wrestling ring. He runs right at me, screaming, 'Chaaaaaarge!'

I turn to Jack, laughing at what a crazy brother he has, and Barney headbutts me hard, right in the place that boys do not want to be headbutted. I howl, double over in pain and drop to my knees.

'Barney!' Jack says. 'What've I told you? That area is strictly off limits.'

This is the worst pain I've ever experienced.

Worse than when my sister pushed me off the trampoline when I was four and my arm broke in five places. I look up and either I'm seeing double or Barney has spawned a twin.

Barney jumps up on the couch and screams, 'Bonesaw crunch!'

Without thinking, Jack shoves Barney off the couch.

Barney flies face-first through the air towards the large, square sheet of glass that is the Danalis's new coffee table. He travels in slo-mo. Actual slo-mo. I don't think it's just happening in my mind. Barney's eyes and mouth are as round as frisbees. Jack reaches out to catch him but his fingertips only just brush Barney's leg. The slo-mo ends and Barney hits the coffee table hard – very hard.

He shatters it into thousands of tiny, shiny cubes and falls through the frame onto the floor with a sickening thump and a crunch of glass.

Jack and I are frozen in place.

Now I know why those alarm bells were ringing. Why didn't I listen to the bells? I knew this would turn bad. I just didn't know it'd turn *this* bad *this* fast. I start to regain feeling below my waist.

I can hear the whistling sound in Jack's swollen, bleeding nose.

Barney isn't moving.

'Barney?' Jack says, his voice weak.

Nothing.

'Barney-Boo?'

Jack climbs over the frame of the coffee table and kneels down in the shattered glass

next to his brother. He puts his hand on
Barney's back.

'Barney, wake up, little buddy.'

I've never heard Jack be this nice to Barney.
It worries me a bit.

'Is he breathing?' I ask.

'I think so,' Jack says. Then his face changes
from concern to panic, and he sits up straight,
listening intensely. 'Oh, no . . .'

'What?'

'Oh, no.'

'*What*?' But I hear it, too, now – a car in the
driveway.

More specifically, a ute.

Everything inside me turns to water.

'Grab his legs, quick,' Jack says.

I do, and we roll Barney over. His face
has been protected by his Bonesaw beard and

Batman mask. I thought it'd be all cut up. Jack brushes a couple of cubes of glass out of the beard and grabs his brother under the armpits.

A door slams. High-heeled footsteps echo along the path out front.

We shuffle across the lounge room towards the hallway.

We're halfway there when we hear a key in the lock and the front door swings back.

Jack and I stop dead.

Mrs D takes in the scene. She's holding an umbrella over her head inside. Not a great sign.

Her eyes fall on Barney, unconscious, hanging between us.

She's been gone approximately four minutes.

'Mum!' Jack says, all chirpy. 'Hi. What did you forget?'

'What are you doing with my Barney? Why is your nose bleeding and why is Barney wearing his Bonesaw costume?'

Uh-oh.

At least the coffee table is blocked by the couch. I don't think she can see it.

'Well . . .' Jack says.

I try to imagine what's going through his mind. What would be the nicest possible way of saying that we were wrestling Barney, he elbowed Jack in the nose and headbutted me in a very bad place, so Jack shoved him, Barney smashed the glass coffee table with his face and now he's unconscious, possibly dead, and we were just hiding the body?

'We're just . . . giving him a swing,' Jack says. 'You ready, Barney-Warney? Wheeeeee!'

We swing him from side to side and watch Mrs D's reaction. She does not share our enthusiasm.

'Barney *loves* to swing, don't you, Barney?'

Barney does not respond.

'Barney?' says Mrs D, dropping her umbrella and moving in.

Oh no. This is it. The end of our babysitting career. Possibly our lives. Nuts. I was really looking forward to those Mars bars.

Jack and I gently lower Barney to the floor.

'See, here's the thing . . .' Jack begins.

Mrs D kneels at his side, puts her arm under his shoulders. His head lolls back. 'Barney?'

Nothing.

'See, what we were doing . . .' Jack says.

'We were just . . .' I add.

'Barney?' she says again, pushing his mask up, pulling his beard down and tapping him gently on the cheek.

Barney's eyes snap open. 'BOO!' he shouts. He sits up. 'JUST TRICKING! HELLO, MUMMY!' He gives his mum a big cuddle and she topples back onto the carpet with him. They roll around laughing.

'You scared Mummy!' she says.

'Barney funny boy.'

Jack and I watch on, open-mouthed – half-relieved, half-wanting to murder Barney now that we know he's not dead.

'Don't do that again,' she says.

'Just tricking big boys,' Barney says. 'They sooo stoopid.'

'Don't say "stupid", Barney,' she says.

There's an angry horn beep from out front. 'Mummy has to go. Don't trick the big boys again, okay?' She stands and straightens her outfit. 'I left my phone.' She grabs it off the chest of drawers near the front door. 'Bye, boys. Look after Barney. And *no more* wrestling.'

'Okay,' Jack says.

'Bye-bye, silly Mummy.'

She grabs her umbrella, closes the front door after her and clacks off down the path to the ute.

Jack and I slump to the floor against the door as the ute backs down the driveway and heads off up the street. I can't believe we survived. For now, at least. We still have to clean up all the glass. Mr D's Cranky Dad Syndrome is going to go off the charts when he sees what's happened.

'Barney's a trick-ster. Barney's a trick-ster!' he chants, dancing around in front of us.

'That was really mean, Barney,' Jack says. 'We thought you were dead, but still breathing a little bit.'

'Ha!' he says, pointing in our faces and cackling. 'Wanna wrestle?' He wiggles his eyebrows up and down.

Jack and I look at each other, then back at Barney.

'Are you *kidding*?' Jack asks. He glares at Barney, who shrugs his shoulders and looks down at the floor, bottom lip out. 'Absolutely!'

Who Would You Rather Be?

* Wonder Woman or Lisa Simpson?

* The Incredible Hulk or Homer Simpson?

* A meerkat or a giraffe?

* Lionel Messi or Cristiano Ronaldo?

* The lead singer of the most famous band in the world ever or a scientist who cures cancer?

* A tomato or a capsicum?

* A pimple or a wart?

* A genius or a professional sportsperson?

* A snake or a spider?

* A tree or a car?

* The BFG or Willie Wonka?

* A chicken pock or a measle?

* A rabbit or a guinea pig?

* Mr Skroop or Brent Bunder?

* An ear or a nose?

* Snot or ear wax?

* A toe or an armpit?

* A Chipmunk or a Wiggle?

* Donald Trump or Voldemort?

Definitely
Voldemort
for me!

The Last Video Store on Earth

'Seen it.'

'Haven't seen it.'

'Seen it.'

'Haven't seen it.'

Jack and I are at Hollywood Dreams, just like every afternoon. It's the last video store in Kings Bay. The last one in the world, maybe.

We know we can download or stream movies, but Jack and me, we're video store guys. We like talking to Brett, the owner, about movies and how they were made and if the sequel is better than the original and whether he'll give us a free tub of the Ben & Jerry's New York Super Fudge Chunk ice-cream he has in the freezer. (He hasn't yet, but I swear he's on the verge of breaking.)

We like the comforting smell of the shop – stale popcorn garnished with a hint of Brett's feet. He likes to kick off his Converse when he's working the counter. You don't get that smell on Netflix. We like the rundown look of the shop, too – the old, brown timber shelves, the torn '80s movie posters and thick orange shagpile carpet. It's like time travel every afternoon.

'Seen it.'

'Haven't seen it.'

In this game, you have to pick a row in the store and say whether you've seen each movie or haven't seen it. Whoever has seen the most movies in that row gets a point.

'Seen it,' Jack says.

'You have not!'

'I have!'

'We were in here on Tuesday,' I tell him, 'and we did the same row, and you said you hadn't seen it.'

'Yeah, well, my dad hired it on Wednesday, and I watched it.'

'*Zombie Flesh 5*. As if your parents would let you watch it.'

'I watched it from the living room doorway,' Jack says.

'Really? What was it about?'

Jack shrugs. 'Just . . . zombies and stuff. It was pretty boring.'

'You haven't seen it.'

'Have.'

'Haven't.'

'Hey, Brett!' I call out.

He's sitting on his stool at the counter in front of the computer playing Pac-Man. Brett has long, dark, greasy hair and a beard. He's wearing a *Back to the Future* cap and a Goonies t-shirt. I don't think anyone's told him that it's not the '80s anymore. He takes a long swig from a two-litre bottle of creaming soda.

This is Brett.
He's a time traveller
from the '80s

'Did Jack's dad hire *Zombie Flesh 5* on Wednesday?' I ask.

Brett groans and glares at me, but I know he doesn't mean it. He loves me and Jack, really. I mean, who wouldn't? We're adorable. He taps the keyboard. 'Nope. Hasn't been out since September 2003.' He sighs before muttering, 'Like most of the movies here.'

'Thanks.' I give Jack a dirty look.

'Hey, boys,' Brett says. We look down the row of shelves at him. He looks grimmer than usual, which isn't easy. 'I have something to tell you.'

'What?' I ask.

'I've sold the store.'

'What?!'

'Sorry. I meant to tell you earlier. The new owners take over in a couple of weeks.'

This rocks me to my core. Who, apart from me and Jack (if we had any money), would be crazy enough to buy a video store? I thought me, Jack and Brett would grow old together.

'Who?' I ask.

'A couple of businesswomen from Sydney. It's been on the market for three years. I had to sell.'

'Do they know strange facts about movies, like you do?' I ask. 'Do they know that George Lucas's original name for Yoda was *Buffy*? And do they know Yoda was going to be played by a monkey in a costume? You told us that.'

'Well, that's the thing . . .'

'What's the thing?'

'They're not . . . going to keep it as a video store.'

'What?' I spit.

'What's it going to be?' Jack asks.

'A nail salon.'

'What? What's a nail salon?' I ask.

'Where ladies, and probably a few men, sit in big lounge chairs and get their nails polished and stuff. The new owners have a whole chain of them – Totally Nailz.'

'Are you kidding me?'

'The good news is that I'm selling all the DVDs,' Brett says. 'So anything you want, bring some money on Saturday. Grab yourself a bargain.'

'We don't want a bargain,' I tell him. 'We want the store. We want you to be here on your stool, doing Rubik's Cube time trials and saying, "I'll be back!" like Schwarzenegger in *Terminator*. This is our favourite place. What other store allows us to hassle the shopkeeper with a thousand questions for a whole hour, then walk away having only spent a dollar hiring something that will give us *two hours* of fun?'

'Sorry, boys. Maybe you can get your nails polished and hassle the beauty therapist.'

'You can't sell!' I tell him.

'I have to sell.'

'Why?'

'Because I'm forty years old with two kids and I earn less than I did when I was eighteen, and my wife's had enough. No one hires movies from a store anymore. You guys are pretty much my only customers, and you only hire on Dollar Tuesdays, so I'm currently making two bucks a week. The mortgage costs me three hundred.'

'But –'

'Deal's done. I didn't want to tell you but –'

'So, that's it? The end of the line?' I ask.

'That's it,' he says.

I shake my head. I don't feel like I have much energy for 'Seen It, Haven't Seen It' anymore.

'We'd better go,' I say.

'Yeah,' Jack says.

'See you Saturday,' Brett calls as we head outside and pick our bikes up off the path. We wheel them towards home, not speaking, just wallowing in all the bad feelings.

'I can't believe it, the end of an era,' Jack says. 'Who would buy that shop?'

'And a nail salon! It's an insult. People should just bite their nails, not go to a special place to have them clipped.'

'What do we do?' Jack asks.

'What *can* we do?'

'We could try to save it,' he says.

I stop wheeling my bike.

Jack stops wheeling his.

'You are a genius,' I tell him. And in this one rare moment, I really believe that he is.

We high-five and jump onto our bikes, pedalling hard for home.

An hour later we're back outside Hollywood Dreams with our homemade signs. Mine is a broom handle with a large piece of cardboard taped to it. The sign says, 'Save Our Store'. Jack's says, 'DVDs Are the Future'.

We march in a circle out front, chanting, 'Save our store! Save our store!'

'What are you two numbskulls doing?' Brett asks from the door.

'Trying to save your shop from becoming a nail salon.'

'Save our store! Save our store!' Jack and I continue to chant.

Someone beeps their horn as they go past in support of our protest.

'But I *need* to sell,' Brett says. 'I've been trying to sell it for years.'

'We don't care,' Jack says. 'Save our store! Save our –!'

'Boys, please, this is really nice of you, but it's too late.'

'We'll buy it!' I tell Brett.

'Do you have $240,000?' he asks.

'What?' Jack and I stop chanting and marching. 'Someone paid you that much for this place? But it smells like stale popcorn and feet. Did they buy it off the internet without coming to visit?'

'It's a prime position. They're buying the building, not the business.'

'This is our spiritual home. We're not going to let you sell.'

'Save our store! Save our store!'

Another person beeps in support. Or maybe to shut us up. I'm not sure.

'See!' I say. *'Everyone* loves this place. It's the heart and soul of the town.'

'Can you guys knock it off? I don't want the new owners thinking they're buying into trouble. Come in and choose a DVD – you can have it. Take it home right now.'

Jack looks at me, raises his brows. He's keen.

'You can't buy us off,' I tell Brett, waving

my sign at a passing car. 'Save our store!'

'Two!' Brett offers. 'Take two DVDs . . . each. It's my final offer.'

'NO!' I yell. 'We don't want your stinking bribes. Where are we going to hang out? We can't play "Seen It, Haven't Seen It" online. We've tried. It's boring.'

'Boys!' he says firmly. Brett has never spoken to us firmly before. 'It's over.'

I rest the broom handle against my shoulder, and we all stand there in an awkward triangle for a moment.

'What are you going to do?' I ask.

'Get a real job,' he grunts.

'Who would hire you?' I ask.

'Thanks,' he says.

'Sorry, but I thought all you knew was movies?'

'It is, but I guess I'm going to have to learn something else. I wanted to start a movie blog but my wife won't let me. She says there's no money in it.'

'A real job . . .' Jack says, letting the idea sink in.

'That sounds terrible,' I say.

'I know, but what's a guy gonna do?'

'You'll end up a zombie like everyone else,' Jack tells him.

'Yeah, you're a role model to us,' I say. 'A hero.'

'What other adult gets paid to play Pac-Man, drink creaming soda and watch movies?' Jack asks.

'It's been 20 good years,' Brett says. 'In the 90s, Hollywood Dreams was the place to be on a Saturday night . . . practically a nightclub –

nervous people on first dates, brawls over the last copy of *Titanic*. Jack, I think your parents met in the Comedy section.'

I laugh. Jack's dad is the least funny person I know. They should have met in Horror.

'Well, if we have anything to do with it, you'll have another 20 years,' Jack says.

We show up at 7.04 am on Saturday morning. Brett isn't here yet. We slump down in the doorway on the cold concrete and breathe steam. It's 8.15 before he shows. He looks weird. He has little cuts all over his chin, and it looks like he might have washed his hair. I decide, in that moment, to never get married – not if it means bathing and shaving and washing my hair and getting a real job.

'You've changed,' I say.

'Yep. This is the first day of the rest of my life.' He says it like it's the last. 'Are you here to get first dibs on your favourites?'

'Nup,' I say. 'We're here to tell anyone who tries to buy a DVD that it's scratched, and to tell the new owners that the place is haunted.'

'Get out of my way,' Brett says.

He opens up and we step inside for what might be the final time. I look around at all the classic movie posters. I suck in that smelly feet / stale popcorn aroma, hoping to lodge just a little bit of it in my lungs forever.

'How much have you got?' Brett asks.

'Seven dollars and sixty cents,' Jack says.

'I've got $11,' I say.

'Well, knock yourselves out. You have 41 minutes till the doors officially open, and you can afford 18.6 DVDs. I'll round it up to 19.'

So Jack and I have to work out which 19 DVDs out of the 5,000 in the store we like best. I head straight for Comedy and start stacking up Jim Carrey movies. Jack goes for Action and makes a Transformers pile. It's torture whittling down our selections.

At 8.59 am we hand over our cash, Brett opens the doors and 50 people rush in. His eyes go wide with panic. The store is crammed. It's like the Boxing Day sales. I've never seen more than four customers in here before – that's including me and Jack.

People scoop DVDs off the shelves. They drop them on the floor. They tread on them.

'Hey, easy!' Jack tells them. 'Respect the merchandise.'

But they don't listen. They just dump their finds on the counter, hand over a few notes and exit the store, arms piled high with our movies. One guy has *Mrs Doubtfire* in his pile, can you believe it? That's, like, our 22nd favourite film. It only just missed the cut. I try to trip him over in the doorway but he's too quick.

'Boys, I need your help at the register! I'm getting slammed,' Brett calls.

Jack and I scowl at him.

'Please?' he pleads.

We don't want to say yes, not after he's allowed strangers into our home, but it's a pretty important mission. We've never been allowed behind the counter before. And maybe he'll let us press the button to open the cash register drawer. So we do it.

We saunter over behind the counter, trying to make out like this isn't the best thing we've ever been asked to do. Ten or so people have their Leaning Tower of Pisa piles of DVDs lined up on the long counter. They laugh and chat about what a bargain they're getting without any respect for the history of the ground on which they stand.

'Thanks, boys. You've saved my life.'

Jack and I take their miserable money, bag up their movies and, yes, press the button to open the register. I wonder if there are any jobs in the world where you just get to press that button. If so, that's my new life dream.

Brett pays us for our work in creaming soda and packets of chips that went out of date in June 2013. Still remarkably tasty.

If I see someone with a movie I really love, like *Ghostbusters* or the third Harry Potter, I try telling them that it's totally overrated or that the DVD has a curse on it, but people don't care. For a dollar, they say they'll take the risk.

A guy with a really bad mullet buys three sets of our sacred shelves for $20 a pop, and we have to help carry them across the car park to his ute. It's a disgrace. Next, someone'll want to buy Brett's stool. But that's where I draw the line. No way. You don't touch a man's stool.

One lady with big hair, bright red lipstick and a gold watch buys the entire Romantic Comedy section. I bet she'll be a regular at the nail salon once she's sucked this place dry. Although, I must say that I'm pretty happy to see the back of Romantic Comedy.

At 5 pm on the dot, Brett slams the doors behind the last customer and turns around.

Afternoon sun streams in through the front windows, illuminating twenty years of dust stirred up by the moving of the shelves.

The three of us look around at the mostly empty store. Tears well up in my eyes, but I'm too tough to let them spill over.

Nuts. They just spilt over. I wipe them away, as manly as I can.

'Thanks, boys,' Brett says. 'It really means a lot.'

He opens the freezer and grabs the last two tubs of New York Super Fudge Chunk ice cream.

'Here.' He gives us one each.

That brings more tears. 'It must be this dust,' I say, wiping like mad.

'You don't have to help clean up. I'll –'

'It's okay,' Jack says. 'We want to.'

We put the ice cream back in the freezer, and we sweep and sneeze and box up the leftover movies. There are some good ones in there, too – *Spider-Man*, *Hugo*, *Teenage Mutant Ninja Turtles 2: The Secret of the Ooze*.

'Where will all the leftovers go?' I ask.

Brett is on his knees, packing a bunch of Looney Tunes into a box.

'Public library,' he says. 'Any they don't want will go to the tip.'

Jack and I look at each other.

'Or . . .' Brett says. 'You guys wouldn't be interested in taking them off my hands, would you?'

'We spent all our money. And there are still hundreds left.'

'I'll put them on your tab,' he says with a wink. 'Least I can do. You've kept me in business the last couple of years. And kept me company. Annoyed me, at least.'

Half an hour later Mum pulls up out front in her red hatchback. We pile DVDs into the boot, onto the backseat, in the front passenger seat – even the glovebox. We count 826 movies in all. Jack and I are in heaven. Mum, not so much.

Until she sees copies of *Father of the Bride* and *Maid in Manhattan*, her two favourite movies.

As she drives off we stand in the doorway of the shop. It's empty apart from a few shelves, the front counter, the drinks fridge and freezer.

'Thanks, guys.'

'Good luck with your new life,' I say.

'Hey, I got a message on my phone earlier,' he says. 'I went for an interview on Thursday. I think I've got a new job.'

'Where?' we ask.

'The cinema. I'm the new manager.'

'No way! Can you get us free tickets?'

'I knew there was something I forgot to ask in the interview.'

Jack and I laugh and high-five Brett.

We say goodbye, jump on our bikes and pedal off into the darkness towards home.

'This has been the best day of my life,' Jack says.

'No question.'

We spend that night and the next day unpacking the car and setting up half the movies in my room and half in Jack's. Over the next three months we swap DVDs back and forth until we each settle on our perfect collection. We've started a neighbourhood video store with two franchised outlets. We call ourselves The Last Video Store on Earth. And I'm pretty sure we are. Fifty cents a night to hire a movie. Trouble is, Jack and I are our only customers.

But at least every morning I wake up inside a video store. There are tall towers of movies teetering on every flat surface, and I get to play 'Seen It, Haven't Seen It' without even getting out of bed.

TOM WEEKLY'S HANDY HACKS FOR COMMON HOUSEHOLD CHORES

I don't think my mother has ever truly relaxed in her life. She's always DOING something. And that means that she always expects me to be DOING something.

DO MORE BY DOING LESS!

Yay!!

And after a hard week at school, I want to do nothing. (By nothing I mean play video games, eat chips and re-organise my scab collection.) But if she catches me:

a) relaxing for more than 30 seconds, or

b) enjoying myself in any way,

she starts to get ideas. She looks at me like I'm an untapped resource — like coal or natural gas (I have plenty of the latter) — and she will mine me for everything I've got. This is how adults think. They fill every single minute with mindless jobs, like cleaning toilets, vacuuming floors and removing empty chip packets from my undies drawer.

I worry that all this crazy doing-ness is setting me up for a poor work–life balance. What about a little 'me' time? So, I've developed this cut-out-and-keep list of handy tips on ways you can save time, energy, money and, possibly, your life. Now you can do more by doing less.

* It's a proven fact that bed bugs and dust mites prefer a bed that's been *made*. An unmade bed dries out bugs and exposes them to light, frying them in their sleep. So, let's win this war on bed bugs, people.

* Is it really necessary to take all the dishes out of the dishwasher and put them in the cupboard, only to dirty them all up again and put them back in the dishwasher? Let's just call the dishwasher a cupboard with an interesting door and skip the extra workload. And if you're in need of an 'express wash', there's nothing faster than a hungry dog's tongue.

* Why scrub the toilet? In my almost 12 years on the planet, it has never occurred to me to clean the toilet. Just keep the lid down and everyone's a winner. See no evil, smell no evil.

* Soap. Who needs it? Not me. It's made from rendered beef fat and sodium laureth sulphate and sodium benzoate and trisodium ethylenediamine disuccinate

and methylisothiazolinone and coca-midopropyl betaine and cl 42051.
Soap is way scarier than dirt.

* It takes so much time to remove empty bottles and out-of-date cheese from the fridge. Why not just leave them in there? When the fridge is so full of empty packaging and manky, mouldy food that nothing else will fit, simply tip the fridge forward and the empties will slide out. Voila! Fresh fridge. Let's go shopping.

* Wet towels on the bedroom floor? Let's be at peace with this. They soak up dust, stop the floor from getting dirty and save money on new rugs. They can also be used as handy mops if you stand on them and rotate your feet in a circular motion. Let's start to think of the floor as a slightly lower towel rack.

* My studies show that children who don't do homework are 73 per cent happier than those who do. Are we really, as a society, prepared to put work ahead of our children's wellbeing?

Tom Weekly cleaning tip # 17

Just don't look down - EVER!

* Vacuuming? A noisy time-suck that adds at least five bucks a year to the electricity bill and costs me thousands of precious Lego bits. How about we all just agree not to look at the floor?

* Why wheel the garbage bins out every week? Why not leave them on the kerb permanently? You'll never miss bin day again! And if you keep a window of the house open, you can throw banana peels, empty tuna cans and other junk directly from the house into the wheelie bin.

Your basketball skills will improve
and you'll cut down on plastic bags,
potentially saving the world from
destruction.

* Do boys really need to lift the toilet seat
  when they pee? It's so tiring and time-
  consuming, and then we have to go to the
  trouble of washing our hands. Can't we
  just glue the seat into a permanently open
  position and hover for number twos?

* When it's your turn to set the table, try
  telling your brother or sister that it's their
  turn, and then go back and forth arguing
  until your mum or dad finally sets it
  themselves. Problem solved.

If you have any other handy life hacks,
drop me a line at thetomweekly@gmail.com

Attack of the Possums

I open my bedroom door, look both ways
and creep out into the lounge room. My head
thumps and my eyes bulge from my skull after
a sleepless night. I look up and a little scream
escapes my throat. Mum and my sister, Tanya,
are sitting at the breakfast table on the far side
of the room. They look terrifying. You know
how people say, 'I feel like a zombie,' when
they haven't had much sleep? Well, Mum
and Tanya look like *actual* zombies – red
eyes, blotchy skin and a flesh-eating look.

My flesh, I fear. They're wearing dressing gowns and sipping mega-mugs of coffee. The steam rising in front of their faces makes them look even more sinister.

'You didn't fix the roof, did you?' Mum hisses.

'Well . . .' I say.

Not a zombie apocalyse.
Just my family.

'I *told* you to fix the roof.'

'I just –'

'This afternoon. Do you understand me?'
She points a crooked zombie finger at me.

I nod and gulp hard.

Roof. This afternoon. Possums. I make a
mental note and underline it three times.

On Saturday my tennis ball got stuck in the
gutter, up underneath the edge of the roof
at the back of the house. To get it out, I had
to lift a roof tile. I guess I didn't put it back in
place. Jack and I were pegging the ball at one
another, so I was a bit distracted. Last night,
a possum got in – a hundred possums, by the
sound of it.

I hate possums. I know that most people find them cute and it sounds a bit un-Australian of me. I hope the government doesn't find out. I might get deported. I don't like dive-bombing magpies either. I'm not mad on deadly snakes. And as for emus . . .

TOM WEEKLY's
tips for the
ill-informed

possums are NOT cute.
possums are EVIL !!

don't even get me started on emus. I'm glad we don't have an emu in the roof. That'd be bad.

If you're a possum-lover, you clearly don't have one in your roof. Possums in the roof don't just sniff around a bit, find a comfy place to rest their weary possum heads and go to sleep. Roof possums are lunatics. They are pint-sized monsters who threaten our way of life. They wrestle and rumble and fight and growl. They bowl themselves up and down from the front of the house to the back. They invite their friends over and party till dawn. No matter how much you scream or bash on the ceiling with the end of a broom or threaten to make them into a fur jacket with matching hat, they don't stop.

We're just finishing dinner tonight when Mum asks, 'Did you fix that roof this afternoon?'

'Yep,' I say.

'Good. Another night like that and I'll throttle you.'

'I'll do worse than that,' Tanya says.

'Just as well you won't have to,' I say with a smile, and Mum ruffles my hair.

'Good boy. You know what we're having for dessert?'

I shrug.

'Homemade apple crumble. Your favourite.'

'Thanks, Mum.' I take my dinner plate to the kitchen and put it in the sink. I go to the back door and peer through the glass into the cold darkness. There's almost no moon tonight, and I really wish I'd *actually* fixed the roof this afternoon. I can't go out there now. I'd freeze to death. And probably be attacked by an axe-wielding maniac, or a rogue emu. But I feel kinda bad for lying to Mum.

'Crumble's ready,' she says. 'C'mon, my little fix-it man.'

Later, as I drift off to sleep, belly full of crumble, I pray that the possums find some other poor, unsuspecting, almost-perfect child to terrorise tonight. My dreams are restless and rowdy, full of thuds and bangs and skraarks. I wake at 11.59 pm and sit bolt upright in bed. In the dream I was having a possum just fell through the ceiling and landed on my head.

I swipe madly at my face. There doesn't seem to be a possum on it. This is positive.

The house is dead quiet. I listen hard, waiting for the rumble to begin, but there's nothing.

I'm sweaty and thirsty from all the possum-infested dreams. I stumble from my room and out to the kitchen for a glass of water. I take a long sip and stare out the window. I can see my reflection, and I notice two little red lights. And another two. And another. Then it hits me. They're not lights. They're *eyes*.

There are ten or twelve possums staring at me from a tree. A posse of possums. I'm pretty sure one of them is picking his teeth with a long knife. One looks like it has only one eye. Another has tattoos on its pink, hairless snout and bears its sharp teeth, growling in a low, demonic hiss.

I scream but try to swallow it, scared of waking Mum and Tanya.

I have to get to the roof hole at the back of the house before the possums do. I'll fix it and Mum will never know I lied. I carefully place my glass in the sink and slowly edge my way towards the back door, trying to keep their eyes on me so that I can make a run for it before they do. But suddenly they scatter along the branches of the tree. I pull open the door, leap down the steps, run to the corner of the house and clamber up the ladder that I used to get my ball.

I can hear them scurrying along the branch towards me, growling and hissing like something out of a horror movie. I make it to the top of the ladder and reach for the

loose roof tile. I slide it back into place and

bang down hard on it with my fist to make sure it's fixed firmly. And I've done it. Mission accomplished. Mum will never know.

I'm feeling so relieved, until I hear that demonic hiss once more and look over my shoulder to find a dark shadow falling through the air towards me. *Smack!* Bristly fur hits my face. Sharp claws rake the back of my scalp. I grab the possum's wrists, trying to pry the claws from my skin before they reach my brain. Another possum lands on my shoulder. Another on my arm. They rip and tear at my skin. Before I can say '*Possum Magic*' there's one on my chest, my belly and each thigh and calf. I'm covered head to toe in possums. I'm wearing a possum suit.

I scream and start to fall off the ladder. I'm tumbling towards certain death under a scrum of killer possums. This is no way for a man to die. I can see tomorrow's news headlines: 'Boy Meets Furry Fate at Paws of Possums'.

BAM! I hit the ground and, all at once, the wild things leap into the air. I see their silhouettes above me – the black shapes of nine possums flying across the Milky Way. They land and scatter. Within seconds they have scampered up the ladder and onto the roof. One of them slides the roof tile aside.

My possum suit is NOT comfortable.

I think it's the one who was using a machete as a toothpick.

'Hey!' I call.

But it's no use. They form a conga line and disappear into the hole, one after the other, and I'm left lying on the damp grass, my body and head aching from the fall, my skin howling with scratches and nips.

The wild rumpus begins in the roof just as the last tail disappears into the hole.

'Tom!' Mum calls from her bedroom.

I wonder if I'm too young to leave home?

There's a *rumble*, a *tumble* and a *skraark* in the roof.

'*Tom*?' she calls again, closer this time.

Or maybe I'll just take a long, well-deserved holiday. I hear Alaska's nice this time of year.

Thud, boom, bang.

A dark Mum-ish shape fills the back door.

I decide to just play dead. Surely if I'm dead she'll forgive me for not fixing the roof.

Crash, blam, growl.

'*TO-O-O-OM!* Ohhhhhh, how cute!' she says.

Huh? I know I'm cute but it seems an unusual time for her to notice. I open one eye and see Mum coming down the steps towards me. I start to sit up.

'Don't move,' she whispers. 'You'll scare it.'

I feel something nuzzle against my armpit.

Mum is moving in slowly. She takes a sharp breath. 'It has a babyyyyy,' she whispers.

I raise my head ever so slightly to see that one of the possums is snuggling into me. And it has a tiny possum clinging to its back.

'Did you save them?' Mum whispers.

'They love you. You're a hero.'

I hadn't wanted to mention it, but if she says so . . .

Mum kneels down and reaches in slowly to give the possum a pat. I can see the soft, moonlit smile on her face.

Then *SKRAAAAARK*! The possum lashes out and bites her on the finger. Mum screams and the possum bolts off, up the ladder and squeezes beneath the roof tile.

We watch it go. Mum, holding her finger, growls low and husky, kind of like an angry possum. 'I gave you crumble and you didn't fix the roof, did you?'

The possum's tail disappears and I'm wondering if they have space in the roof for one more. Sounds like they're having fun up there.

WHAT PARENTS SAY AND WHAT THEY DO . . .

What they say . . .

'Sugar is bad for you. It rots your teeth. You've eaten too many lollies today. No more.'

What they do the minute you go to bed . . .

Bust out the world's largest block of chocolate and stuff their faces with it. When you get up to go to the bathroom and catch them, they tell you to 'mind your own business' and continue to scoff the block.

Oh honey, sugar rots your teeth.

What they say . . .

'No more screen-time. You spend your whole life staring at a screen. When I was a kid we climbed trees and caught tadpoles.'

What they do . . .

Continue checking social media and 'work' emails on their phone *while* they say this to you.

What they say . . .

'I'm putting your device away FOREVER for what you've just done. You are NEVER having it back. I'm throwing it in the bin!'

What they do . . .

Secretly watch Netflix on it at night in bed because it's way better than their own iPad.

What they say . . .

'Stop shouting!'

What they do . . .

Shout this at you.

What they say . . .

'I'm vegetarian.'

What they do . . .

Eat fish and eggs and when you ask them what's the difference between eating a cow and eating a fish or an unborn chicken they mutter something about cows being man's best friend and chickens being stupid.

What they say . . .

'No, you can't have lemonade! You've had enough sugar. It's a "sometimes" drink.'

What they do . . .

Take another sip of their own 'sometimes' drink.

What they say . . .

'I expect you to get an A in that maths exam this morning!'

What they do . . .

Hide their own dodgy school reports and exam marks in a lockable vault in the back of the shed, claiming they must have lost them when they moved house.

What they say . . .

'Eat your breakfast. It's the most important meal of the day.'

What they do . . .

Drink coffee for breakfast and tell their friends, 'I just can't face food in the morning.'

Mum's breakfast
(best to avoid her until she's had it)

What they say . . .

'You should read a book. Reading is good for you.'

What they do . . .

Turn the page on their Bunnings tool catalogue or trashy celebrity magazine.

What they say . . .

'It's important to speak to people respectfully, with kindness and understanding.'

What they do . . .

Reach up to the top shelf of the pantry and scream, 'I'm going to murder whoever ate all the Tim Tams!'

The Christmas Kiss

'It's going to be the best Christmas ever,'
Mum says.

She puts the white beard over my head
and I feel the elastic snap tight to the back of
my scalp. She pulls my red hat with the furry
white trim down over my brow. 'You look
great. Now, get out there and impress those
judges.'

I take another bite of candy cane. (I've
already eaten 12 tonight, a personal record.)

'This is so embarrassing.'

'You have nothing to worry about. We've practised the dismount a dozen times. You'll do great,' Mum says. 'C'mon, off we go.'

She opens the front door and I peer through the fly screen. I can see the big Christmas tree lit up in the middle of the yard. There's a neon Santa and snowmen. Strings of lights outline the front porch, trees and bushes. Six white boomers are frozen in mid-leap over the front fence, and there are hundreds of plastic candles, toy soldiers and snowflakes all over the yard.

It's Christmas Eve and, somehow, Mum has tricked me into helping her try to win the Kings Bay Festival of Christmas Light contest. She's always wanted to enter. The judges are down on the front lawn near the road with about 50 other people.

I can see my best friend Jack down there next to the family of penguins with top hats. And Mum's friend Andy, the Kings Bay *Echo* newspaper photographer, is standing next to them. He's come to take a shot of Santa arriving. Most importantly, I can see my wife-to-be, Sasha – the whole reason I agreed to do this humiliating stunt.

Sasha's obsessed with Christmas, too. When I told her that Mum wanted me to dress up as Santa and deliver candy canes and Christmas puddings to everyone on our front lawn on Christmas Eve, she thought it was the greatest idea ever. I told her there was no way I was doing it, and you know what she said? 'If you do it, I'll kiss you.' My jaw dropped. 'On the cheek,' she added. But I was in no position to make demands. Sasha. Kiss. Deal.

So, here I am, putting my reputation on the line for the woman I love.

sigh..

The things you have to do to get a kiss...

I pat my fat pillow belly, and a little bit of candy-cane-flavoured stomach acid shoots up and burns the back of my throat. Mum shoves open the screen door and ushers me outside. 'Off we go.'

'Hey, look! Santa!' a little kid yells. A couple of camera flashes go off.

'Oh, yeah, Santa!'

More flashes.

Mum guides me to the balcony railing where the zipline starts. It runs down past the Christmas tree, over the neon Santa and six white boomers, over the front fence laced with fairy lights and onto the strip of grass next to the road where the crowd is gathered.

It's a warm night and I realise I'm sweating up my Santa suit. My belly doesn't feel too good either with Mum's lasagne, a bucket of fear and 12 candy canes swirling around in it.

'I don't know if I want to do this anymore.'

'You'll be fine,' she tells me. 'Remember how well you did in practice? It's the same thing but with a Santa suit on. Off you go. Judges are waiting. They can't hang around all night.'

I grab hold of the zipline handle.

'He's coming down!' a little girl yells, clapping her hands. 'Santa's coming! Santa's coming early!'

I can't help smiling. There are whistles and cheers.

'Your public wants you, Mr Claus,' Mum says.

I climb up on the verandah railing and sit with my legs hanging down, Santa sack over my shoulder.

A chant starts up from the crowd. 'San-ta. San-ta. San-ta!'

I scan for Sasha and, when I find her, she's staring right at me with those blue-sky eyes. I imagine what my cheek will feel like with her lips attached to it.

'Off you go,' Mum says, shoving me in the back. 'Good luck!' I slip off the railing and start down the zipline, slowly at first, my sweaty hands clutching the handle and the Santa sack, feet dangling down.

'Whoooo!' the crowd cheers.

Kids' excited faces are lit up by the Christmas lights. Dozens of phone-cameras flash-fire. And one big flash from Andy, the *Echo* photographer. Sasha, the girl of my dreams, and my best mate are down there waiting for me. I feel like I'm inside a dream as I glide over the reindeer, candles and toy soldiers.

Adrenaline kicks in as I start to pick up speed.

'San-ta. San-ta. San-ta,' the little kids and parents continue to chant.

They love me. Sasha loves me. And my mum is going to win the Festival of Christmas Light. I know it.

I zip past the Christmas tree, but I feel a little tug on the back of my Santa suit. I look back to see that a string of Christmas lights has caught on my thick black belt. I reach around to unhook it. As I do, my Santa sack slips from my hand and the contents spill all over the grass beneath me, setting off a mad scramble from a bunch of the kids. I'm hanging by one hand from the zipline handle, my white Santa gloves losing their grip. The lights attached to me are rapidly tearing away from the tree and trailing along behind me like a long tail.

Crunch.

My boots hit neon Santa and his head snaps off, sending sparks and shards of glass flying. The sparks shoot up my legs and I feel a rush of heat as the white fur on the bottom

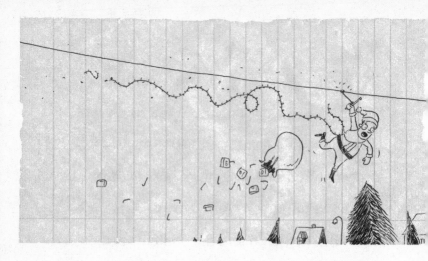

of my Santa pants catches fire. I scissor-kick
my legs but the air movement seems to fan
the flames, giving off black smoke and a
plastic stench. I'm almost at the front gate
when I feel the electrical wire that's hooked
onto my Santa belt snap. There's a loud *bang*
and all the lights in the yard go out. So do the
street lights. And the neighbours' lights across
the road. I think our street just won the Kings
Bay Festival of Christmas Darkness. There
are screams and howls. I'm plunging through
the dark towards the gathered crowd, and the

only light now is my rapidly spreading pants-fire.

Sasha and Jack's faces are illuminated orange and wide with fear when, *smack*, my flaming boots hit Jack right in the chest. He topples to the ground. I land with a *thump* next to him and skid to a hand-grazing stop on the gravel at the edge of the road.

'Put him out, put him out!' someone yells.

I roll over in an attempt to extinguish my pants when I'm hit with a wall of water. I squint through the spray to see the silhouette of a man hosing me down. He has a clipboard in his hand. It's one of the judges. Seconds later, the fire is out and my steaming legs start to cool rapidly.

'Thank you,' I sputter.

I realise that most of my pants are missing,

revealing my polka-dot boxer shorts and stick-thin, slightly chargrilled chicken legs.

Sasha reaches down to give me a hand. Others gather around, staring at me.

'Are you okay?' she asks, helping me up. 'Your poor legs.'

'I think so,' I say. 'Bit hot. Scorched, actually.'

She holds my hand, pulls me close, takes off my Santa beard and leans in to kiss me on the cheek. There are a couple of 'woots' from kids nearby.

I'm so excited that my belly spasms with the shock of it. I feel the candy canes' acidic warmth rise in my throat again, and I go to cover my mouth . . . but I'm too late. A stream of red, white and green candy cane goo streams from my mouth, onto

Sasha's t-shirt and down onto her jeans. Andy from the *Echo*, like any good journalist capturing a dramatic moment, takes two quick photos.

A squeak of disbelief escapes Sasha's throat. She looks at me, horrified.

Season's Greetings!

I wipe my chin and go to say sorry –
at least my breath is nice and minty – but,
as I open my mouth, I hurl again, on her
shoes this time. Sasha shoves me in the chest,
shrieks, 'Oh my God!' and races off through
the crowd. She mustn't have realised I was
about to apologise.

'Sasha!' I scream, but my voice is hoarse
with acid burn and it comes out in a whisper.
'Sasha!' I try again, but she's gone and I'm left
standing there in the dark.

'Bummer,' Jack says, standing up from
where he was lying on the grass a couple of
metres away. He rubs his chest where my
flaming boots hit him. 'You owe me a new
Captain America t-shirt.'

Mum arrives on the scene and says,
'Are you okay, Tom?'

I can't tell if she's concerned about
my health or annoyed that I've wrecked
everything.

I give her an evil glare. *No, I'm not okay.*
What part of me looks okay?

Mum turns to the Festival of Christmas
Light judge who's still holding the hose.
He looks like he's in shock. He drops his
clipboard.

'Thanks for putting out my son,' she says.
'How did we do? Apart from the fire and
blackout, I mean? And all the vomit. Tanya,
grab a mop! I actually have a replacement set
of boomers in the garage. Do you think we
have a chance of winning?'

She looks hopeful.

Acknowledgements

The Tom Weekly books are super-fun to write.
I love the cast of misfit characters that has developed
over six books. I have many people to thank for their
contributions. Firstly, my publisher Zoe Walton,
editor Brandon VanOver and illustrator Gus Gordon,
who contribute so much to the series. Thanks
to Laura Harris, Dot Tonkin, Zoe Bechara, Tina
Gumnior, Angela Duke and the rest of the team at
Penguin Random House Australia, who help transport
the books from my brain into kids' hands. I'm forever
grateful for the support of Jo Butler and Anthony
Blair from Cameron's. And the booksellers, teachers
and parents who inspire kids to read.

A huge thanks to you, the readers! The story
'Hostage' was inspired by a comment about a guinea
pig by a Year Six student at Gordon East Public

School. I then developed the story by brainstorming it with kids in lots of different schools and festivals across Australia. I love allowing readers into the writing process. I try to include these ideas wherever possible, although some of them are too crazy even for Tom Weekly.

Here are the kids and schools who contributed to these brainstorm sessions in class and on Instagram: Bryce, Isaac, Georgie, Harry, Abbie, Daisy, Liadan, Dale the Whale, Charlotte, Max, Olivia, Tigist, Mercedes, Tabitha, Cameron, Edward, Tommy, Hugo, Ben, Alyssa, Jayden, Ashley, Corey, Nimna, Eliza, Alice, Noah, Zooey, Oscar, Andy, Jordan, Claire, Kayla, Abbey, Josie, Natalie, Tayla, Jakob, Emy, Aidan, Will, Cayley, WatchMeetMake, Ebi, Micky, Woody, Lucy, Lochie, Alaria, Cherry, Lilly, Hamish, Brett, Miro, Liam, Lucas and Talulah.

Thanks to the kids at Scotch Oakburn College

Junior School, Launceston Church Grammar,

St Thomas More's Primary School, Varsity College,

Sheldon College, St Pius X, Ambrose Treacy College,

Churchie, Seaforth PS, Five Dock PS, Emmanuel

Anglican College, Ballarat Grammar School,

Greenacre PS, Riverbank PS, Grand Avenue SS, West

Pennant Hills PS, Chipping Norton PS, Nuwarra PS,

Our Lady Help of Christians Parish School,

Newington College, Saint Stephen's College year 6,

The Gap SS, Boronia Heights SS, Yugumbir SS, Aitken

College, St Catherine's Wishart, Sholem Aleichem

College, Shelford Girls' Grammar, Leibler Yavneh

College, Marymede Catholic College, Assisi Catholic

College, Wilson's Creek PS, Durrumbul PS, Empire

Vale PS, Wyrallah PS, Holy Family Catholic PS,

Nimbin Central School, Cabbage Tree Island PS,

Eureka PS, Bangalow PS, Alstonville PS, Crabbes

Creek PS, Murwillumbah East PS, Joan of Arc

Catholic PS, Woodburn PS, Broadwater PS, Uralla Central School, St Mary's Catholic College, Brisbane Boys' College, Oakhill College, Warrawee PS, Willoughby PS, Bardia PS, Jindalee SS and the kids at Byron Writers Festival's Kids Big Day Out.

Thanks again to Millie, Jack, Hux, Luca, Gem, Cosmo, Iggy, Maggie, Sol, Bridie, Trinity, Lulu and Scarlett for 'What Would You Rather Do?' dreaming and to Jaron and Cody for their feedback on 'Razorblade Fruitcake'. Thanks to Mrs Faulconbridge's class for feedback on 'Attack of the Killer Possums' and to my friend Andrew for almost being eaten by possums and inspiring the story.

I can't wait to take this book out in the world and share it with kids everywhere. I hope it inspires you to create your own stories. Your life is full of them.

About the Author

Tristan Bancks is a children's and teen author with a background in acting and filmmaking. His books include the Tom Weekly series, Mac Slater series and crime-mystery novels for middle-graders, including *Two Wolves* (*On the Run* in the US) and *The Fall*. *Two Wolves* won Honour Book in the 2015 Children's Book Council of Australia Book of the Year Awards and was shortlisted for the Prime Minister's Literary Awards. It also won the YABBA and KOALA Children's Choice Awards. Tristan is a writer-ambassador for the literacy charity Room to Read. He is excited by travel, mountain biking, the future of storytelling and inspiring others to create. Visit Tristan at tristanbancks.com

About the Illustrator

Gus Gordon has written and illustrated over 70 books for children. He writes books about motorbike-riding stunt chickens, dogs that live in trees, and singing on rooftops in New York. His picture book *Herman and Rosie* was a 2013 CBCA Honour Book. Gus loves speaking to kids about illustration, character design and the desire to control a wiggly line. Visit Gus at gusgordon.com

Room to Read®

About Room to Read

Tristan Bancks is a committed writer-ambassador for Room to Read, an innovative global non-profit that has impacted the lives of over ten million children in ten low-income countries through its Literacy and Girls' Education programs. Room to Read is changing children's lives in Bangladesh, Cambodia, India, Laos, Nepal, South Africa, Sri Lanka, Tanzania, Vietnam and Zambia – and you can help!

In 2012 Tristan started the Room to Read World Change Challenge in collaboration with Australian school children to build a school library in Siem Reap, Cambodia. Over the years since, Tristan, his fellow writer-ambassadors and kids in both Australia and Hong Kong have raised over $100,000 to fund children's education in low-income countries.

For more information or to join this year's World Change Challenge, visit tristanbancks.com/p/change-world.html, and to find out more about Room to Read, visit roomtoread.org.